MY FIRST MISTAKE

SADIE KINCAID

For all my wonderful readers who are looking for some cozy Christmas feelgood spice, Chase Hunter is here to make all your filthy dreams come true,

Love Sadie xx

CHAPTER 1

ADDISON

 # Never date a guy who calls you Sugarmuffin

I stare at Jasper's face unblinking. Has he always had that mole right beneath his left ear? Can't say I've noticed it before. Although his beard is a little shorter than usual. Either way, he should probably get that checked out.

"We're just in different places in our lives, Adders," he says in that annoyingly saccharine voice he adopts whenever he's trying to get me to agree with something I absolutely shouldn't—like the time he wanted us to have sex in the cemetery, right before we were caught

1

by Sheriff Nolan, or when he convinced me to invest in his microbrewery. Both my dignity and two thousand dollars I'll never get back.

But his voice drags me back to this living hell that is my present situation. The smell of sex still lingers in the air and I balk.

"Oh, Adders," he says again, tone dripping with fake concern. It has to be fake because if he had any genuine concern for my wellbeing, I'm pretty sure he would *not* have been nailing his new side-chick on my couch.

I hate that any part of his weed-addled brain might think that I just violently retched because of anything remotely connected to his imminent departure from my life. I also hate that he calls me Adders. My name is Addison. Addie. Adds or Ad if you're not into multiple syllables, but never Adders. I'm not a snake, unlike my soon-to-be-ex-boyfriend.

He makes a sad face. "Lacey just gets me, Sugarmuffin."

Lacey? The woman he met last week at a Renaissance fair who is currently in my bathroom, probably cleaning his cum from between her thighs, or off her boobs—he was always obsessed with jerking off on my boobs. *She* gets him? Wait until she has to let you move all of your things into her apartment because you lost yet another job when you got high while you were supposed to be watching the security monitors. Then we'll see how much she gets you. I clamp my lips together and don't say any of those things.

The fact that I caught Jasper banging Lacey on *my* couch and in *my* apartment isn't even in the top five things that are bothering me right now. Our relationship has been over for months. But like a wilting orchid, I have continued to feed and nurture it in the hope that it would hold on—just until the end of winter. Not because I care about said relationship, of course. Jasper is handsome, and charming when he wants to be, but he's also a sleaze who will bone anything with a pulse and has an overinflated sense of his own importance. The latter was evident by our sixth date. I would have dumped him after the fifth one if I'm honest, but Jasper had two crucial things in his favor. One being that he didn't grow up here in Juniper Ridge, and two being impeccable timing. Not only was he actually with me when I got the call about Braxton and Eva's imminent winter wedding—one so imminent that my mom is convinced there's a grandchild in her near future—but he was also free on the date in question. And, sure, I might have been using him just a smidge, but he did get free room and board out of the deal—not to mention all of the other fringe benefits.

I only needed nine more days from you, Jasper! Two

hundred and sixteen hours where you didn't put your dick in someone else.

Lacey emerges from my bathroom, pulling her blue faux-leather mini down. She flashes me an apologetic smile. I should warn her not to invest in any of his get-rich-quick schemes, but I can smell my favorite Jo Malone perfume, and I'm far more annoyed that she helped herself to my Pomegranate Noir while using my bathroom than I am at her helping herself to my boyfriend. *That* is all on him. So, I don't offer any words of advice. Petty? Yes. But I figure I've earned it.

"I'm sure she does get you, yeah," I mumble, while mentally going through the name of every guy I've ever dated and wondering if I can convince them to come to a wedding with me in five days' time. Pretty sure even if they were single, their answer would be no. My relationships don't tend to end amicably, and I have a history of picking guys who are the most epic kind of wrong for me. Many have gone on to find very fulfilling relationships, so I'm well aware that I'm likely the problem. Too much—or not enough.

Jasper rests a patronizing hand on my shoulder. I expect he intends it to comfort me somehow, but it only makes my skin crawl. That I put up with him for five long and torturous months and allowed him to treat me like garbage is a testament to how desperate I was to have a date for my brother's wedding.

And now that dream is disappearing faster than Jasper's hopes of becoming *a leading light in the world of microbreweries*, right before my very eyes. Dammit! My lip wobbles.

"Oh, Adders," Jasper repeats, still with that sickly sweet tone.

Oh, dear God, he really does think I'm upset about him.

"Please just go, Jasper. I'll box up all your things and leave them outside. You can pick them up whenever you have time."

"I'm really sorry, Sugarmuffin." He pulls an even sadder face.

I'm not, asswipe.

But I feign a sad smile and open my front door, ushering him and his new Renaissance-fair girlfriend out of it.

"Oh, by the way, your toilet is blocked. I flushed a condom," she says with a nonchalant shrug of her shoulders.

"Good to know," I force out the words and close the door behind them. Then I rest my forehead against the cool wood and curse my stupid life.

I need to call Emma. She'll know what to do. And even if she doesn't, she'll at least drink with me until I can no longer feel my face—and then hopefully I will no longer be forced to stare into the abyss that is having to face Chase goddamn Hunter as the desperately lonely single girl he left behind eight years ago.

CHAPTER 2

CHASE

**# Never agree to share a secluded cabin with a
woman who once threatened to drive a stiletto heel
through your heart**

"Y ou're a genius, Chase. I mean, I never thought
anyone would be able to bring my vision to
life, but you've...dammit, son, I don't know
how you did it, but it's perfect."

I smile at the face of Gregory Chambers on my
computer screen—one of my newest clients, who's just
visited the site of his ecologically friendly and fully self-
sufficient twelve-story office building in Dallas for the

first time. My VP, Claudia, along with the site foreman, Isaac, are with him, and they're both beaming too. I'm only sorry I couldn't be there myself. The excitement when someone sees their dream come to life is infectious and it never gets old—at least if we do our jobs right. "We're just glad you trusted us with your baby, Mr. Chambers. It's been a pleasure to work on a project so close to your heart."

"And there's no one else I would have trusted with it. Like I said, genius." He laughs like he's giddy with excitement.

"I just design the building, my people on the ground actually build it. They're the real geniuses."

He places his hand over his heart. "You're all incredible in my book. Seriously, I'm blown away. The board are thrilled with the progress, and our staff can't wait to move into our new premises."

"Always got to keep your staff happy, right?"

Gregory nods and Claudia and Isaac give each other a knowing smile. I pride myself on looking after my staff—and not only because it makes good business sense to cultivate a happy, healthy and loyal workforce.

"And are we on schedule for completion mid-January, Isaac?"

My foreman nods. "Sure are, boss. There are a few

snags for you to fix but nothing that will delay completion."

We make a little small talk about Gregory's plans for Christmas and then I end the call. As soon as I'm done, my assistant, Keeley, comes into my office.

"Your out of office is all set up, but I'll keep a close eye on any urgent matters and update you accordingly." She places some papers on my desk. "The final contract came through from the Ontario Group for your attention. And so did the response from the cable company regarding the Lansing apartment complex."

Keeley has been my personal assistant for four years and she knows I prefer to read actual papers than words on a screen.

"Your flight to Vermont is booked for eight a.m. tomorrow morning and I took the liberty of arranging you an airport hotel because I know how much you hate having to get up at the *ass crack of dawn* in winter."

Another thing she knows about me. I think Keeley might be the longest relationship with a woman I've ever had. That's probably both fucked up and also not unusual in my world. Building a multi-million-dollar business from the ground up kind of eats into a person's social life.

"Thank you, Keeley. I don't know what I'd do without you. I should give you a raise."

She smiles sweetly, knowing she's due one in January anyway. "Yes, you should. You could also give me the whole week of New Year's off. Christopher has finally invited me to meet his parents."

I arch an eyebrow. "Christmas in Paris?"

"Except his parents live in Boulogne," she reminds me with an eye roll.

"Surely a deviation to Paris is called for though? I hear it's the most romantic city in the world."

She puts her hand on her hip. "Does this mean you'll give me the time off?"

I pretend to mull it over, but the truth is, her boyfriend, hopefully soon-to-be fiancé, has already asked me and I already approved it weeks ago. Christmas and New Year's are always slow and I'm the only masochist who doesn't take any time off over the holidays. "I guess I can live with that, providing you make me one of your incredible coffees before I leave."

Her eyes light up and she throws her arms around me in an uncharacteristic display of emotion. "You're the best boss ever."

I pat her shoulder gently. "Yeah, thanks. Now go get my coffee. I have a trip to pack for."

"Chase, I need you to do something for me," my best friend, Braxton, says as soon as I answer his call.

I give a brief nod of acknowledgment to the bartender who places my glass of bourbon on the bar. She offers me a flirtatious grin and then gives her ass an exaggerated sway as she walks away to serve another customer. "Anything. As the best man, isn't that kind of in my job description?"

"This one isn't exactly in the job description, buddy." I can picture him scratching his beard, twisting it into a knot beneath his chin that way he does.

"I'm sure I can handle it. Shoot." I take a drink of my bourbon, certain there is nothing my best friend of twenty years could ask me to do that I'm incapable of. He's been my ride-or-die since we were ten years old.

"I need you to share a cabin with Addie at the wedding."

I swallow the amber liquid before I choke on it. Okay, there is *one* thing he could ask me to do. "And why do I need to share a cabin with your kid sister?"

He sighs. "Well, for starters, she's not a kid."

Yeah, and don't I fucking know it.

"And, she just broke up with a guy and she's..." He pauses, probably not for dramatic effect knowing Brax, but it sure adds to the tension.

11

"She breaks up with guys all the time. *All* the time, Brax," I remind him before he can finish his sentence. And then I clamp my jaw closed and silently curse myself for revealing that I know such information about his sister. I haven't been home to Juniper Ridge in eight years, and I therefore shouldn't know anything about Addison Kinsella's dating life—yet I do. I know everything.

"Yeah, and I get that, but it seems this guy was different."

Jasper—the loser who can't hold down any job longer than six weeks because he can't get his ass out of bed on time—was different? I swallow my incredulity and work to keep my voice calm. "Different how?"

"Well, I never thought he was any different from the rest when they were dating. They sure lasted a couple of months longer than her usual strays. But she never seemed all that into him to be honest..."

Good! He was a fuck-knuckle who didn't deserve her. I smile and take another sip of my bourbon.

"But, well..." He blows out a breath. "Eva saw her in the bar a few nights back, and she was...she was really cut up about this guy dumping her."

"Addie was dumped? And she was cut up about it?" I believe neither of those things, but I have no reason not to believe Eva—Braxton's bride-to-be and the girl who used to puke her guts up whenever she told a lie back in high school and was therefore both one of the worst and best friends ever.

"I know. I would never believe it myself, but she was crying into her goddamn wine."

"She was drinking wine?" Addie is a neat bourbon kind of woman, and she only drinks wine when...well, when she wants to *get all in her feels.* Another random fact I shouldn't know about her.

"I know, buddy. I told you it was serious. She's acting like she's okay now, of course. Classic Addie. But now we have to go to Vermont and obviously she and that douche had a cabin of their own, so now Addie will be in a cabin in the middle of nowhere all by herself. There are no spare rooms in any of the shared ones. And for some reason she chose the one farthest away from the lake. I dunno what's going on with her but I'm worried about her, Chase. And you're the only person I trust to look after her."

No, she chose the one farthest away from *me,* not the lake. I am the one person he shouldn't trust to look after her, and I am certain Addie would be in full agreement with that assessment. But of course, neither she nor I will ever tell her overprotective brother the reason why that is. She's never forgiven me and I can't say I blame her, but she's never ratted me out either. "Surely, there's someone else she can room with? A bridesmaid? A distant cousin?"

"She's our maid of honor and only bridesmaid, as you know, buddy," he reminds me. Eva was never one for making a lot of friends, neither male nor female. Brax and I were always her people, and then Addie too as she got older. And Brax has no female relatives he's particularly close to other than his mom and sister, so of course there are no other bridesmaids. "And our cousins are all sharing with someone or in couples," he adds.

I remain silent. Surely, there's a better option than me?

"So, you'll do it, yeah?" Brax asks.

What? Spend four whole days in a tiny cabin with the walking bundle of sass, fire and seduction that is Addie Kinsella? That will be torturous enough, but then there'll be the nights too. Nights when she'll be in the room next door to me...Fuck, she'll kill me in my sleep. Or she'll torture me instead. Put itching powder in my boxers. Sew shrimp into the lining of my tuxedo.

"Chase?" Brax snaps me out of those thoughts.

For the love of fuck! I one hundred percent cannot do this. "Of course, Brax. Anything you need."

"Thanks, buddy. I'll see you tomorrow, yeah."

"Yeah." We say goodbyes and end the call and I down the rest of my drink.

Tomorrow!

That means less than twenty-four more hours of freedom before I have my balls metaphorically, and quite possibly literally, skewered by Addie Kinsella. Although I haven't seen her in person for eight years and maybe she won't still hold a grudge. There have been some unavoidable video calls with Brax and Eva for wedding prep, or when she's been at their place over the holidays, or when they've been visiting me in LA and have called her. Those latter occasions, when I've said a quick hey, and then made a big thing about giving them space, while I secretly remained in earshot just so I could listen to them talk. Which inevitably reminded me of all the things I miss about Juniper Ridge. During all of those calls, she has been her usual bright and bubbly self. However, even in the heat of the LA sunshine, I could feel the ice in her tone whenever she directly addressed me. Or maybe I imagined all of that. Perhaps she's mellowed since I left. Maybe she's no longer the raven-haired firecracker who told me she'd drive a stiletto through my heart if I ever set foot in Juniper Ridge ever again. Perhaps she's forgiven me?

And now I'm officially certifiably insane.

I signal for another drink and the same bartender serves me again. I'm only vaguely aware of her telling me what time she gets off and asking me if I have a room here in the hotel. I mumble an excuse about being on a flight in a few hours and then head to a quiet corner of the bar. Ordinarily, taking her up on her offer would be a no-brainer. But now Addie is in my head, and as usual, she refuses to fucking leave.

CHAPTER 3
ADDISON

 # Never let your soon-to-be sister-in-law find you crying into your wine nine days before her wedding

I hold the wild jasmine to my nose and take a deep inhale. It's one of my favorite scents in the entire world and it never fails to make me smile. Then I carefully place it into the Wild Bloom arrangement I'm currently making for Edith Calhoun. Her husband, John, gets her a bouquet of flowers every other week without fail, and they almost always include wild jasmine.

My soon-to-be sister-in-law, Eva, is supposed to be selecting the final flourishes for her wedding flowers—they'll be artificial flowers, of course, so they still look fresh in five days' time and can be reused afterward. The latter being particularly important to Eva who likes to recycle everything. These particular flowers will be donated to Juniper Ridge's nursing home to spruce up their Christmas décor, and I'll add some extra holly and mistletoe to ensure they look as festive as possible once I'm back from Vermont. But instead of looking through the various samples of eucalyptus and ferns, Eva's eyes are burning into the back of my skull. Her concern for me is mildly suffocating, not to mention entirely unnecessary.

"Are you sure you're okay?" she asks again, her usual soothing tone only making my skin prickle today.

I screw my eyes closed, give myself a quick reminder that she's only concerned because she's like my big sister and she loves me, plaster a smile on my face and spin around.

"I'm fine, Eva. No, I'm better than fine. I'm great. And more importantly I'm excited for your wedding," I say, trying to direct her back to our important job of choosing the greenery that will be added to the table decorations to her winter wedding in Vermont.

Her eyes narrow in suspicion, and I can hardly blame her after she found me wasted in Rogue's bar a few nights ago, crying into my rosé and telling her my life was over. How dare Jasper Bolton dump me five days before we were supposed to leave for my brother's wedding?

Ordinarily, I wouldn't give one solitary hoot. I'm too busy for a relationship and I love being single—it's my natural state of being. But *now*, I have to attend my brother's wedding as a one with no plus. And that is a fate worse than death. Not even because my aunt Irene likes to loudly ask me when I'll find a nice guy and settle down, but because of *him*. Chase Hunter. My brother's best friend and best man—the latter being a moniker that has never been so thoroughly undeserved. Worst man. Breaker of hearts. Betrayer of trust. Stealer of virginity under false pretenses. All of those titles would be much more appropriate.

"You sure you don't want to drive down with us?" she asks.

I scoff at the notion. "Play third wheel to you and my brother while you fondle each other in the front seat for six hours. Ugh. No thanks."

She smiles sweetly and then her warm hands are cupping my cheeks. "I worry about you driving alone at night, Addie. Is that so bad?"

"I'm twenty-seven years old, Eva. I've traveled around Europe alone, I think I'm perfectly capable of getting to Vermont. As I also had to remind Mom and Dad this morning before they left at the butt crack of dawn. Besides, I need room for all of your beautiful flowers."

Her brown eyes fill with concern. She doesn't care a lot about the flowers; she's not a flowers kind of gal. But she cares about me, and she always supported my dream of opening my own boutique flower and gift store one day. "You know I love you, right?"

"Yes. And I love you too." I raise a brow. "But I still don't need to witness the lovefest that is you and my brother at such close quarters. It's frankly sickening how much the two of you can't keep your hands off each other." This is an outright lie and she knows it. The truth is, the two of them are adorable together. They've been best friends since they were thirteen, but it took them fifteen years to realize they were supposed to be together, despite it being clear as day to everyone around them. And I couldn't be happier for them.

She wrinkles her cute button nose. "Well, what if I promise we won't *fondle* in the front seat the entire way there."

"Still, I'll pass."

She sighs. Defeated.

"Hey." I catch her hand in mine and squeeze. She's always been there for me, even before she and Brax were an item. She was there to comfort me on the worst day of my life, even if she doesn't know the reason why it was so awful. "I know you're worried about me, but I promise you I'm fine. The other night was just a..." I search for the words. It was what? An existential crisis brought on by the reality that I'm about to see Chase Hunter for the first time in eight years and I'm not sure whether I'm going to kick him straight in the balls or fall into a crying mess at his feet? No, best not tell her that. "You know how I get when I drink wine. I am not heartbroken over Jasper, I swear to it." I hold up my hand like I'm swearing allegiance to the flag.

Her piercing brown eyes narrow on my face again. She's too shrewd for her own good, my soon-to-be sister-in-law, or definitely too shrewd for mine. "Maybe not. But there's something going on with you."

I roll my eyes.

"I'm not going to push. I trust that you'll tell me when you're ready. Just know I'm always here and I would never ever judge you. Okay?"

"Hard to judge someone who's wiped up your vomit and tears when you drank an entire bottle of tequila after Brax got engaged to that yoga instructor from New York," I remind her. Their love affair was brief and very misguided, but it broke poor Eva's heart.

She gasps loudly, feigning her indignation. "Yeah, well you promised me we would never discuss that again."

I pull her into a hug, wrapping her in my arms and holding on tightly. "I love you. I'm excited to watch you marry my doofus big brother. I'm okay. Really." Or I will be once this wedding is over and Chase Hunter goes back to his fancy penthouse apartment in LA. Then normal service will be resumed.

"Okay." She steps out of my embrace. "I have to run. But we'll see you for drinks tonight, right?"

I nod. "I should get in around ten and I'll meet you at the bar in the main lodge."

She smiles, still failing to hide all of that big sisterly concern in her worried expression. "I'll have a large bourbon with your name on it."

"I'd expect no less."

Eva gives me a final hug goodbye and shouts a farewell to Emma who's hiding out in the storeroom at my request, and then she's gone.

Perhaps I should have told her what happened all of those years ago and then maybe I wouldn't be feeling so much dread about what is sure to be a truly wondrous occasion. But then she probably would have thought less of Chase. And then she would have felt torn between her loyalty to him and her loyalty to Brax and me, and then maybe the three of them would no longer be the best of friends. And I couldn't be the one responsible for that travesty, because it surely would be one.

No, I did the right thing. And I'm a big girl now. Not the naïve nineteen-year-old college sophomore who thought the sun shone out of Chase Hunter's perfectly toned ass.

Emma comes out of the storeroom, mischief sparkling in her tawny brown eyes—exactly the reason I asked her to make herself scarce while Eva was here. "Why the hell don't you just tell her the truth? You and she are pretty tight." She steps around the counter and bends to tuck her long, trailing lace into the side of her bright purple Dr. Marten boot. "She could be the perfect wingwoman for you this week. You know, seeing as how you won't take me as your plus one."

"I don't need a wingwoman," I reply defensively. "And I can't take you because someone needs to take care of the store. Besides, the only thing sadder than showing up at Brax and Eva's wedding alone, is showing up with my employee."

"Rude!" She crosses her arms over her chest. "Would *an employee* know the real reason you had tears and snot running down your face the other night at Rogue's?"

I almost regret telling her about Chase and me, but Emma is one of the few people around here who didn't grow up in Juniper Ridge, having moved here three years ago after college, and as such she is immune to the charms of Chase Hunter. The rest of the town, including my brother and his wife-to-be, remember the star quarterback with the perfect white smile who would stop his car to help an old lady cross the road. They remember the good guy Chase pretended to be. Unfortunately, I know the truth behind the charm and dimples.

I pinch the spot between my brows and take a breath. "You know you're way more than an employee. I'm sorry, Em. I'm just feeling so on edge."

"I know, girl." She wraps a comforting arm around my shoulder. "All the more reason you should tell your brother what a heartless, disgusting douchebag his bestie actually is."

I offer her a faint smile. If only it was that easy. Because the truth is, Chase is a good guy, at least for the most part. He's always been there for Brax. When the bank almost foreclosed on his repair shop, it was Chase who bailed him out. When my idiot older brother got stranded in Budapest with no money to get home, Chase didn't just wire him some cash, he sent a private jet to bring Brax home. He even sent Brax a sympathy card when his dog, Huxley, died. He is a good guy, just not to me. I can't believe that I wasted a second of my time on him. But we all make mistakes, it's just that mine happened to be a huge one that broke my heart into a billion pieces. "I can't do that. I can't ruin their friendship, not to mention Brax and Eva's wedding."

"Looks like you're gonna have to suck it up for the next four days then, girl. Brutal." She shivers dramatically.

Who even has a wedding that lasts four damn days? Brax and Eva would have gotten married in the little church in town, but Eva's mom insisted on a big white wedding at some fancy lodge hotel in Vermont for her only child. One that will be packed full of festivities that are gonna last for four freaking days! As the sister of the groom and chief, aka only, bridesmaid, I can't even duck out of any of it. But I do have a plan.

"I made sure to get the cabin that's farthest away from the main hotel lodge, which is where Chase will be staying. In public, we'll be civil and polite, and then I'll never have to see him again. It will be fine." I'm impressed that I at least sound convincing.

Emma snorts a laugh. "Good luck with that." Then she nudges me in the ribs, her eyes twinkling like she has an idea. "But you could hook up with one of the other groomsmen. That would really piss this Chase guy off, huh?"

I shake my head. "Not gonna work. Cole and Oliver are married, and Parker is gay. Anyway, I'm sure Chase wouldn't notice. He'd barely bat an eye if I walked down the aisle beside him naked."

Emma gives me a dramatic eye roll. "Even Parker would notice you naked, Adds. I've seen you in a bikini, remember? So maybe that's what you focus on? You rock your bridesmaid dress, and every other outfit you wear this week, and show this Chase dude what he's missing."

Also not going to work. He knows exactly what he's missing, and if he missed it at all, he'd have come back here at least once in the last eight years.

CHAPTER 4

CHASE

 # Never tell your best friend the real reason his sister hates your guts

T tip my Uber driver and grab my suitcase before heading into the hotel. I tried to call Brax and Eva after my flight landed but the cell signal here is awful. I'm hoping he's had a rethink about the whole me staying with Addie thing, even though I know that's as likely as snowfall in hell. He adores his kid sister, and he will absolutely not stand for her being heartbroken and alone in some cabin.

Nor will I.

Dammit!

I head into the hotel and straight for the bar. The place isn't my usual taste, but it's nice—rustic with its own certain kind of charm. The walls have been designed to appear like they're made of logs and the faint scent of pine only adds to the log-cabin feel. Thick flannel tartan drapes hang in every window, and portraits of bears and wolves pepper the walls.

There are a few people here but none that I recognize, so I go order a bourbon and wait. The last text Brax sent me said he'd be here by four and it's a little after that time now, so I'm sure I won't be alone long.

"Well, look who's here. My favorite little thief." I recognize Brax's mom's voice immediately and when I spin on my stool, she's standing there with a huge smile on her face. I slip off my seat and she stands on her tiptoes, wrapping her arms around me and enveloping me in a cloud of her sweet-scented perfume, the one that brings me straight back to my childhood.

"How long are you gonna hold that whole apple incident against me, Maggie?" The first time I met her was when she caught me stealing apples from their backyard. She gave me a clip around the ear and then sent me home with an entire bag for my mom. I was ten and it was a day that changed my life, because it was also the day I met Brax. I hug her back tightly, basking in the familiarity of home, even if we're far away from

Juniper Ridge. But after my mom died when I was twenty-one, the Kinsella family are the only family I have left, and they will always be home to me.

"Oh, you know I like to keep you on your toes," she chuckles.

"Hey there, son." Jack Kinsella claps me on the back. "How's about them Rams, huh?"

I place my hand over my heart. "Now, Jack, you know my heart will always bleed red, white and blue."

He laughs—a die-hard Patriots fan like me. "That's my boy."

"Huunnteeeer!" Brax's voice fills the bar room now. He extends the vowels of my last name the same way he always has, so it sounds like a battle cry.

Maggie rolls her eyes and not a few seconds later, I'm being wrapped up in everything that is Braxton Kinsella. I hug him back just as fiercely. Fuck, I've really missed him. "It's been too long, buddy," I mumble against his shoulder.

He squeezes me tighter, because he knows. No matter how far apart our lives have taken us, he's always been my ride-or-die, and he always will be. I'm stoked to be here for his wedding, even if I'm decidedly un-stoked about having to endure four days in a cabin with his sister. However, given that she hasn't blown up my phone or my social media, telling me she'd rather freeze her ass off in the snow than share a cabin with me, I'm assuming she's taken the news of our lodging situation relatively well. And it's not like we'll be sharing a bed or anything. Although I'm not gonna lie, that thought did cross my mind last night, and it was not an unwelcome one. I blame it entirely on the half bottle of bourbon I drank though. Entirely.

"Chase! What took you so long?" Eva sidles up to us now and Brax steps back and allows me to hug my other best friend—his very soon-to-be wife.

As soon as I let her go, he has his hand on her ass and then they kiss each other like they've been apart for months rather than mere minutes. Maggie and Jack excuse themselves to go meet some distant family members and I'm left alone in the company of the lovebirds.

"You two really should get a room, you know?" I feign my disgust, but actually I love seeing the two of them together. I always told Brax that Eva was the one for him, and I'm glad he finally realized that for himself.

Brax rolls his eyes. "You sound like Addie."

Ah, Addison. My eternal tormentor. "Speaking of Addie, I assume she was okay with the whole cabin-share situation?"

His mouth drops open and he slaps his forehead. "Fuck!"

Well, this can't be good. "What do you mean, fuck, Brax?"

He screws his eyes closed and mutters the word fuck at least another half a dozen times.

"Please tell me that you've told her I'm going to be her roomie for the next week," I plead with him, but already I can tell by his face that he hasn't. And that, of course, would explain the lack of any hostility from her regarding the situation. Stupid of me to assume she might have forgiven me after all these years. Even though, if I'm honest, I don't want her forgiveness unless I've fucking earned it, because that will mean she's moved on. And maybe that's the real reason I've never tried to apologize, because as much as it might make me an asshole, it would fucking kill me if she moved on.

"I...fuck! It totally slipped my mind."

Eva nudges him in his ribs. "You never told me either. I could have let her know this morning when I was at the store."

He slides his arm around her waist and kisses her cheek. "Sorry, babe, with all the wedding prep, I completely forgot about it."

She flutters her eyelashes. "It's okay, I forgive you."

I don't though. Addison doesn't know we're sharing a cabin this week. Fuck! "Slipped your mind? You know she's going to go apeshit when she finds out, don't you?"

He scoffs. "She'll be fine. You're practically family. Like her big brother."

I am definitely *not* like her big brother. She really never told him a single thing about me and her, did she? "She is Addison, buddy. She's gonna be pissed that you sprung this on her. And yeah, we might have been close when we were younger, but we haven't been in the same room together for eight years and now we're sharing a cabin, you do realize that, right?" I scrub a hand over my face.

"Chase is right. You need to call Addie right now and tell her," Eva chides him. "At least to stop her from braining him with a frying pan if she thinks he's an intruder."

She's more likely to brain me for being me than an intruder. She'd probably have an intruder sit down, offer them some tea and ask them what went so wrong in their life that they had to turn to crime.

Brax fishes his cell phone out of his pocket and then he dials Addison's number. The signal is so poor here it takes him a few tries to connect, and all the while the heavy feeling of dread is growing in the pit of my stomach. Eventually he gets through. "Addie. Addie!" he yells into the phone.

"Can she hear you?" Eva asks.

He nods. Then he loudly tells her that she'll be sharing a cabin with me for the next four days.

With a triumphant smile, he tells her he'll see her later and ends the call.

I stare at him. "So, what did she say?"

"She was fine," he assures me.

"What did she say, Brax?" I repeat, because there is not a chance on God's green earth she just took that news well.

"She said she'll see us all later." He smiles again, but it's unnerving.

"She couldn't hear you, could she?"

His grin turns distinctly sheepish. "There's a small chance she didn't hear a single fucking word I said, but I have every confidence that she did," he declares.

I am seriously rethinking my decision to agree to his ridiculous request. "Maybe I should just stay at the main lodge like I originally planned."

He shakes his head. "Can't now, buddy. Eva's mom moved some people around and there are no other rooms available."

"Then I'll sleep on a sofa in the lobby."

He slaps me on the back and lets out a throaty chuckle. "I know Addie used to be a pint-sized tyrant, but she's cool now, buddy. You guys will have tons of fun catching up."

"Brax, I..." I swallow the words. Now is definitely not the time to confess how I broke his baby sister's heart by being the biggest jackass on the face of the earth.

His eyes narrow and his expression changes, filled with concern. "I don't want her out in that cabin all on her own, Chase. I know she can take care of herself, but I'll just worry about her, especially with the shitty cell signal. And I know she might be a little blindsided to find she's sharing a cabin with you, but I'll tell her it was all my fault. Please, buddy?"

He knows I can't resist the puppy-dog eyes, and even if I could, I hate the idea of Addie being out in a cabin in the woods all alone just as much as he does. She's so damn trusting, she'd probably welcome a Sasquatch in for supper if one knocked on her door. "Fine. But you owe me. And if she punches me in the face, then don't blame me for me having a black eye in your wedding photos."

Eva links her arm through both mine and Braxton's and guides us toward a table on the other side of the room. "Addie would never hit you. I bet she's super excited to see you again."

I highly doubt that. "What time is she getting in?"

Eva chews on her lip. "She said ten."

I nod. It's six now so that gives me plenty of time to shower and change and be back here at the bar in the safety of witnesses by the time she arrives. Then Brax can explain our living situation in front of dozens of people, who can testify at my funeral that I really didn't deserve to go out that way. Then, I'll ply her with bourbon and hope she gets so drunk she passes out before she can stab me through the heart with a stiletto.

Eva laughs softly. "Remember back in high school when she had that huge crush on you. It was so cute."

I remember all too well. It *was* cute when she was a kid. And then she wasn't a kid. I left for college and every time I came home she was less kid and more blossoming siren. I never had a single impure thought about her though. Not one. Not until I came home the Christmas after she'd just turned eighteen—and bam! She was very much a woman. A stunning, sassy, smart-as-fuck, wears-her-heart-on-her-sleeve woman. A lethal combination of dangerous and innocent. My kryptonite.

CHAPTER 5

ADDISON

\# **When bumping into a semi-naked ex who trampled on your heart, never ever look at his man meat**

T check my watch and feel a wave of panic. "Dammit. Dammit. Dammit!" I'd hoped to be on the road by three so that I could get to the cabin by eight and then have ample time to freshen up and put on my best game face before I have to see Chase in the flesh. And now it's almost four already.

"Damn flowers," I grumble, stuffing the last of the table decorations into the trunk of Angelina—my stunningly beautiful, bright-yellow Volkswagen.

Of course, it's not the flowers' fault that I'm late, that's entirely due to my indecision over what to pack for this four-day adventure into hell I'm about to embark on. I really should stop referring to my brother and practically-already-my-sister's wedding that way, but I can't help it. The thought of seeing Chase in person makes me want to simultaneously vomit and explode into a fit of rage. And I'm not totally sure which one of those events is most likely to happen. Actually, it would probably be the former knowing me.

Space in my little car is limited, so therefore what I packed had to be limited too. And while I know I should have opted for the comfortable and sturdy boots, and only *one* pair of heels for the wedding, of course I opted for four pairs of truly stunning heels and no boots, other than the ones on my feet. Because heels make me feel confident and sexy, and I'm going to need all the help I can get in that department.

When the final box of flowers is in the car, I wedge the trunk shut and then squeeze my suitcase onto the passenger seat, nestling between more flowers.

And then I roll back my shoulders and give myself a much-needed pep talk. This trip is going to be awesome. I'll get to spend time with my parents, whom I adore, see my two favorite people in the entire world get married and catch up with some cousins I haven't seen for years. Plus, I'll get plenty of time to myself to do all the things I barely get time to do, like read and meditate—the latter being something I've never done in my entire life, but which Emma keeps telling me would be good for me. I even downloaded myself an app to give me some pointers.

Yes, this week is going to be perfect!

I'VE ONLY BEEN DRIVING for a few miles when I get a call from Brax.

I answer it, but I can barely hear him.

"Brax, is everything okay?"

"Ad...bin...ter...kay." Broken pieces of words are all that come through.

"Brax, I can't hear you. I think your cell signal there is awful," I tell him, because my dashboard says I have full signal.

He goes on talking, but the sounds make no sense. He's all jumbled up now, like a robot speaking an alien language.

"I'll be there by ten," I shout, as though that might miraculously help him to understand me.

The line goes dead and the car is filled with Mariah Carey's angelic voice once more. I sing along and can't help but recall those times I sang this song into my hairbrush, imagining how one Christmas I would get exactly what, or who, I wanted—Chase Hunter! Just goes to show you should be careful what you wish for, huh?

THANKFULLY, the drive to Vermont has been straightforward and stress free so far. And I should arrive with enough time to brush my hair and my teeth, and then change into something that doesn't make me look like a florist. Not that there's anything at all wrong with looking like a florist—I am one after all—but jeans, a flannel shirt covered in lily pollen and sheepskin boots aren't exactly the look I'm going for this week.

I follow the directions to Lakefisher Lodge, which to my relief is very well signposted. I chose this one because it was the lake cabin farthest from the main hotel where the wedding is being held, my reasoning being I wanted to be as far away from my past as possible. It was only when I looked at the pictures online that I realized why this particular lodge was so far out of the way. Jasper was thrilled to discover what the second bedroom was used for, even though I assured him we'd be getting zero use out of it. I snort a little laugh at the look on Emma's face when I showed her.

"Wow! People in Vermont sure like to get their freak on," she'd said.

I reminded her that people everywhere liked to *get their freak on* and what better place to do it than a secluded cabin in the woods. I actually feel a little sad for the place that it will be getting zero action of any kind this week. I did bring my vibrator though, and a new set of nipple clamps I'd hoped to try with Jasper but will no doubt be happier testing out alone. But still I'm sure Lakefisher Lodge is used to far kinkier and more exciting action than anything I'm going to do this week.

I'm surprised to find the lights on when I pull up to the cabin. But what a nice touch. It makes the place look warm and welcoming, and I suppose also ensures that any guests don't trip over or bump into anything if they're arriving in the dark.

I grab my suitcase from the front seat and then fire off a text to Eva, telling her I've arrived and I'll meet them in the bar after a quick shower and change. There's a path that leads directly from Lakesfisher Lodge to the main hotel and I have a flashlight, so I have no qualms about finding the place. I get a little red warning error telling me my message didn't send.

Damn phone signal. I hold my cell up in the air, like that might help, but of course it doesn't. It will be fine.

She's expecting me around ten and *around* ten is when I'll be there.

I enter the code on the email I was sent and retrieve the key from the little locked box before letting myself in. Immediately, something feels wrong.

Why the hell does this place smell like cologne? Why is there steam coming from one of the bedrooms?

I shriek when the silhouette of a man appears in the bedroom doorway, grabbing my suitcase and holding it in front of me like a shield, like it would do me any good at all, but still, a girl's gotta use whatever she has to hand.

"Addie?" That voice is so achingly familiar, and also so very rage inducing.

I drop my suitcase with a thunk. "Chase? What the hell are you doing here?"

He holds up his hands in surrender as he steps out of the room and into the light. Damn asshole is wearing only a towel, slung low on his waist. Low enough to see the V that disappears beneath it...My gaze drifts lower.

No, Addie! We do not admire Chase Hunter's physique, no matter how pleasing to the eye it might be, and we definitely do not look at his man meat. Never.

"I can explain," he says, walking toward me.

I snarl. If I had my heels on, I'd brandish one like a weapon and tell him to get the hell out. "I'm pretty sure there is no logical explanation in this entire world that would explain you being here, half naked, in *my* cabin."

"Brax was worried about you and he asked me to stay."

Ah! I guess there is *one* explanation. "And you agreed to, why?"

"Because he was worried you were brokenhearted over some douche-canoe and he didn't want you spending four nights in this secluded cabin on your own. And to be frank, I don't really like the idea much myself. There's not even any decent cell signal here. And the Wi-Fi is shocking."

I snort. "Don't pretend you did any of this out of the kindness of your heart, Chase. Leaving aside the fact you don't possess one, you did this because Brax gave you an impossible choice. And you didn't want my brother to find out what a giant ass-face you truly are."

He sucks in a breath, hands on his hips as he glares at me. "Like I said, he was worried about you. And your broken heart, apparently."

"I do not have a broken heart," I snap. "Far from it. You, though, almost had a broken face. You could have given me some prior warning that you'd be here. I almost had a heart attack. What if I'd been carrying a gun?"

"You hate guns."

"Still, if I *didn't* and I *had* been packing heat, I could have shot you right in the ass or something."

I'm sure his lips twitch like he wants to smile, but he doesn't. "Brax tried to tell you earlier but like I said the cell signal here is awful."

"So, you just invaded my cabin without even asking? How did you even get in here?" I dangle the cabin key on my finger.

"Eva's mom explained the new situation to the hotel desk and they gave me an extra key."

"And then you decided to wander around half naked to jump out and surprise me? And I see you already chose a bedroom. So, you just walked in here and took over *my* cabin that I paid for with no thought for anyone but yourself?"

He rolls his eyes. "I didn't *choose* any room, Addie. I just took a fucking shower in the first bathroom I found. You can have whatever room you like. I really don't give a shit."

Clearly, he didn't look around when he got here. I fold my arms over my chest and look him dead in the eye. "You're sure about that?"

He nods. "Yeah."

Oh, well, at least this next part is going to be so much fun. It might even be worth the horror of having to share a cabin with him for the next four nights. My

43

shock at finding him here is quickly being replaced by sheer delight. It's probably very wicked of me, but still... he deserves it.

I suppress a snicker. "Shall I show you where you'll be sleeping, Chase?"

He frowns now, confused and wary. "If you insist."

"Oh, I insist. Shall we?" I indicate he should follow me along the hallway, ignoring how much I like the scent of his cologne when I get within a few feet of him. Does he have to smell so good? Can he not have one thing that helps me be repulsed by him—aside from the fact he's a heartless asswipe, obviously? But unfortunately, my hormones don't appear to react to that quite as sensitively as they do to his inappropriately intoxicating scent.

I can no longer keep the grin from my face when we get to the cabin's second bedroom and I push open the door—revealing a state-of-the-art sex dungeon, complete with blacked-out windows, blood-red painted walls, an entire wall of floggers, whips and handcuffs and the pièce de résistance—a swing hanging from the center of the ceiling.

"What the actual fuck?" Chase's shocked gasp makes me giggle, and I press a hand over my mouth to stifle it.

He steps into the room, spinning around with his

mouth hanging open. "What the fuck is this place, Addie?"

"I believe the brochure describes it as an 'Aladdin's cave of sexual pleasure that will satisfy all your needs.'" I lean against the door jamb. "Surely, you've seen a sex dungeon before, no?"

His eyes land on mine, his face a delightful picture of confusion and horror. "What. The. Fuck?" he says again.

"Your vocabulary has seriously diminished since you moved to LA, Chase. You said that already."

He ignores the barb. "Why the hell did you book a cabin with a sex dungeon?"

I could tell him that the sex dungeon was inconsequential and the location was its only selling point, but he doesn't need to know that. Instead, I steel myself and roll back my shoulders. "Why do you think?"

He winces, like he's disgusted by the idea of me having sex or using any of the equipment in here. Of course he is, because I'm his best friend's annoying kid sister. The one he *threw a bone* to. Why would any guy want to do anything like that with me, huh? That painful memory claws its way to the surface and I push it away. This should be about enjoying the look on Chase's face as he realizes he'll have to sleep on a sex swing.

"I mean, it looks kind of comfy. Like a hammock?" I offer.

He runs a finger over one of the leather straps and wrinkles his nose. "I wonder how many people have fucked on this thing?"

Ugh. I don't want to think about that actually.

His eyes lock on mine and they narrow a little, enough so I notice. "If you're going to fuck on a sex swing, Addie, you should really consider getting one of your own."

What now? My knees tremble. "What makes you think I don't have one? Couldn't exactly pack it up with all the flowers and bring it, could I?"

His jaw tics. "I guess you won't be needing either this one or your own this week now."

Asswipe! Obviously, he knows I just got dumped. I wish he also knew that I'm not even a little sad about it, and I don't need his pity. "I guess not."

He glances at the swing again. "Looks like I'll be sleeping on the sofa then."

I snort. "Looks like. I'll think about you when I'm lying in my three hundred thread count Egyptian cotton sheets and curled up beneath the goose-down duvet."

He arches a brow. "Oh, I have no doubt you'll be thinking about me, Firefly."

Firefly? How dare he use that cute little pet name for

me after everything he did, but hang on, what? Why is he being so cocky...Dammit! "I didn't mean..." I screw my eyes closed. I want to face-palm myself, but I take a breath and work to regain my composure. When I open my eyes again, he's staring at me with a wicked grin on his face. "My only thoughts about you, Chase Hunter, are...very not nice." Wow! Way to go, Addie! Burn!

He laughs darkly. "Hmm, I expect they're real naughty."

What! Holy firecrackers I need to get away from him. He turns my usually sharp brain into a blunt instrument. Maybe it's the abs. Or the cocksure smile. Or the outline of his...

"You wish, asshole!" is the snappiest retort I can think of, that along with turning on my heel and removing myself from his orbit.

I will survive these next four days.

I will not fall for Chase's easy charm.

I will not stare into those bright blue eyes and remember how good of a kisser he is.

I will not make another Chase-Hunter-sized mistake.

CHAPTER 6
CHASE

 # Never ever question a woman's choice of footwear —no matter how inappropriate

That went much better than I expected it would. She didn't try and stake me through the heart, or the balls, and while the night is still young and there's time for both of those things to happen, I'm pretty sure she's more pissed at her brother than at me. Or maybe it was my shocked reaction to the sex dungeon which really softened the blow for her. No wonder that guy on the reception desk was looking at me funny when I told him which cabin I was staying in. A heads up that it was a sex den would have been nice.

The fuck I will be sleeping in there though, and I'm trying my best not to think about her and her fuck-knuckle ex doing anything in that room. Because then I'll think of him putting his hands on her, touching her, making her moan, and then I'll get so angry I'll probably punch a hole through the sex dungeon wall. *Or* I will think about me and her in that room instead, and all of the filthy things I could do to her, and that's even more dangerous.

So, I stare out of the window and wait for her to get dressed. Not that she asked me to wait, in fact, she specifically told me to go ahead without her, but I'll be fucked if I'll let her wander through these woods on her own.

Twenty minutes after she went into what I now know to be the cabin's only bedroom, she emerges again. Gone are the jeans and flannel shirt, which she looked cute as fuck in, and in their place are a black dress, the kind that covers her skin but reveals every delicious curve. I try not to let my eyes rake over her greedily, but I can't fucking help it. And then I get to her feet, and the black stiletto heels.

Fuck me! These next four days are going to be torture on so many levels. "Do you really have to wear those ridiculous shoes?" I ask her, and by ridiculous, I mean I can't stop myself from imagining what they'd feel like if her legs were wrapped around my waist and those heels were digging into my ass.

"These are Louboutins," she says, lifting the heel to show me the distinctive red soul. "And they are not even close to ridiculous."

"They are when we're walking a quarter mile through the woods."

She frowns. "There's a path though, right? The brochure distinctly said there was a path."

"Yeah, there's a path, but what if..." I scrub a hand over my face. I can't exactly tell her I'm going to spend the entire walk imagining what it would be like to pin her against a tree and fuck her while she's wearing nothing but those shoes. "What if we get attacked by a bear or a really angry beaver?"

Her lips lift in a faint smirk and she rolls her eyes. "Don't worry, I'll protect you if we do." Then she struts across the room and I am certain that she sways her hips and ass on purpose. Siren.

"I'm not carrying your ass back here if you get drunk on bourbon tonight," I call to her already retreating back.

She slips on her coat, flips me the bird and then sashays out of the door.

~

"ADDIE!" Brax's triumphant cry echoes through the bar as soon as she and I walk inside. He runs over and pulls her into a bear hug, squeezing her tightly. She squeals with delight, hugging him back with as much force. Even if she's pissed at him because of our roommate status, she can't help but mirror his excitement. They've always been close and I love seeing them together. It always makes me wonder what my life would have been like if I'd had a sibling, especially after Mom died. "Hey, doofus!" she says.

"Fart-brain," he murmurs. "I'm so glad you're finally fucking here."

He releases her from his embrace and she slides off her coat. "Me too. Although a heads up about my surprise guest would have been nice."

Brax winces, glancing at me like I can help him out, and I shake my head because I absolutely cannot. "I'm sorry. I forgot to tell you, and then the cell service was fucking shit, and..." he blows out a breath. "I didn't want you out on your own in that cabin. Eva would never forgive me if some lumberjack came and carried you off to his lair." He grins.

She grins back, and he's already forgiven. I've seen the two of them have some epic fights before. One time Addie tossed a whole bucket of ice water over him right as he was headed out to a date with Ruby Holland, the girl he'd been asking out for months, just because he'd used the last of the hot water. But they never stayed mad at each other for long. They always have each other's backs, no matter what. If Brax knew what I'd done—how badly I'd hurt her—I'm pretty sure he'd never forgive me, and that realization has guilt flaring hot in my chest.

"Hi guys," Eva joins us, carrying two glasses of bourbon. She hands one to Addie and the other to me.

Addie downs hers in one impressive gulp, before smacking her lips together in satisfaction. She and Eva hug like long-lost sisters, and then Eva says something about her dress being perfect and thanking Addie for the shoes, and the two of them jump up and down excitedly.

Brax watches them both with a smile on his face and I realize I'm doing the same.

"Addison Kinsella, did I really just see you inhale that glass of bourbon in front of all these people?" Maggie cuts in.

Addie rolls her eyes and then spins to face her mom. "I was thirsty, Mom. I've been driving for over five hours. And then I almost had a cardiac event when I walked into my cabin to find a half-naked man prowling around."

Again with the half-naked accusations. "Hey, I was

not prowling," I say, my free hand raised in defense, or perhaps it's surrender.

Maggie pops an eyebrow. "But you *were* half naked?"

"I was not *half naked.*"

"So, you were full-on nude?" Maggie gasps.

"What? No!"

"Chase! You hound dog," Eva chides me, her lips twitching in a smirk.

"Why the fuck were you naked in my sister's cabin, dude? Do I need to kick your ass?" Brax asks.

I look to Addie for some support, so that she can confirm I'm not some creep who was hanging around her cabin in my birthday suit waiting for her arrival, but her eyes are sparkling with mischief and her lips are pressed together like she's trying to stop herself from laughing.

And now I realize they're all yanking my chain, because these people trust me, and they assume I would never take advantage of her like that. And I don't even have the brain space to unpack any of the guilt I feel over that right now. "Like you could kick my ass," I tell Brax.

He shrugs, like he doesn't care that he can't.

"I had just gotten out of the shower and I was wearing a towel," I explain.

"What's going on here?" Now Jack joins our little party.

"Chase was prowling around Addie's cabin half naked earlier," Maggie informs him, deadpan.

The man does not flinch at this revelation, not even a little. He just accepts that it cannot possibly be true or maybe that Addie was okay with it—at least I assume he does, because he once threatened one of his daughter's dates with his shotgun after he made her cry. Jack simply gives Addie a kiss on the top of her head and tells her he's happy to see her. Then he pats me on the back and ushers us all to a table.

Fuck, they really have no idea, do they? Addison never told any of them a thing about what happened between us, and clearly nothing about what a piece of shit I was after. And for that, I will be eternally grateful to her.

THE LOOK ADDISON is giving me could melt steel, I'm sure of it. I can't blame her though, as best man and maid of honor/only bridesmaid, the two of us are almost like celebrities tonight. After she caught up with her family, she and I were accosted by Eva's mom, who insisted on introducing us to every person here. And despite us repeatedly trying to put some distance between us, we seem to end up being drawn into the same conversations. The only saving grace is that half of the wedding party are yet to arrive, and so we're only being told we make a really cute couple, or putting up with the best man hooking up with the bridesmaid jokes from fifty or so people, rather than a hundred.

"If one more person asks me if we're going to hook up, I think I might vomit," Addie says through clenched teeth.

"Just one more hour and then I'm sure we can call it a night," I offer.

She groans, expertly dodging her handsy cousin, Kelvin, and diverting him toward her mom. "A whole hour."

"Would bourbon help?"

"Yes. Very much."

I give her a mock salute. "Then your wish is my command."

She flips me the bird again, but she also smiles at me. And this time, there's a hint of sincerity in it. It's the kind that could knock a man on his ass if he's not careful.

CHAPTER 7

ADDISON

 # Always be humble—the universe is watching and she has a wicked sense of humor

"Are you sure you can walk in those shoes?" Chase asks, incredulous as we make our way along the path back to our cabin.

"I can walk in heels better than you can walk in your bare feet, Hunter," I tell him.

He hums, staring at me, with either concern or awe before he admits, "Yeah, you can."

I don't know what that tone of voice is about, but it makes me feel a little wobbly inside, so I ignore it and I try to ignore him, but the annoying asshat keeps talking.

"You've loved ridiculously high heels for as long as I can remember. Why?"

Well, now I have to acknowledge him. "Why? Seriously?" I stop walking and lift my right foot. "Just look at this bad boy. It's freaking beautiful."

He smirks. "I can't argue with that, but I mean, don't they hurt your feet or something?"

I shake my head. "No. They fit like slippers," I lie with ease. The truth is, these ones are pinching my toes like a mofo right now, but I'm accustomed to the discomfort. "I don't wear them for comfort; I wear them because of how they make me feel."

"Oh? And how is that?" He seems genuinely intrigued.

"Confident. Badass," I tell him honestly, revealing far too much. But perhaps I'm a little more buzzed than I thought I was. "It doesn't matter how crappy about myself I might be feeling, or how nervous about an event, or whatever, I slip these on and I feel like a different person."

He's staring at me, bemused.

My cheeks flush with heat and I feel stupidly embarrassed now for admitting that. How can someone as perfect and good at everything he does ever understand something like that? "It's crazy, I know," I babble.

"No, not crazy at all. I get it. I have a lucky suit that makes me feel like that."

"No, you do not!"

"Yeah. It's Dolce and Gabbana. Custom made. Whenever I have a big meeting or there's a client I really want to close a deal with, I always wear it."

I blink at him in shock. "I would never have pegged you as a lucky-suit kind of guy."

"And why not? Don't most people have a lucky something?"

"Yeah, but you're not most people, are you? You're Chase Hunter. Perfect at everything. Gets whatever he wants with a click of his fingers." I really didn't mean that to sound quite so snarky as it did, and the look of hurt that flashes over his face makes me regret it instantly.

His jaw works. "Not everything, Addie."

The sadness in his eyes tugs at my heartstrings, because unlike him, I have one—and now I feel guilty. "I didn't mean...I was trying to say you're good at everything, but I..." Ugh, why is this so difficult? "I know how hard you work."

He doesn't answer and now I'm feeling progressively more like an insensitive asshole while desperately trying to think of something to say that will lighten the mood again. And I'm so distracted by that that I don't see the rock until I'm tripping over it. Luckily, I manage to put my hands out to stop me from falling flat on my face and attending my brother's wedding with a busted nose or a black eye, but I twist my ankle and my hands hurt.

"Addie!" Chase yells, sounding worried.

"Ow!" I whimper.

"Fuck, are you okay?" He asks and before I can stop him, he's scooping me up into his arms and holding me tight to his chest. Even in the dim lighting that illuminates the path, I can see the concern in his eyes. And now I feel like a prize idiot. Boasting about how I can walk in my heels and then falling over—that's what I get for bragging. Thanks universe!

"I'm fine," I insist. Despite the pain in my ankle, my pride is hurt more than anything else. "Put me down."

"The cabin's not far. You might have a sprain or something."

"I don't. I can walk on my own, Chase." I almost sob out the words because he's being so nice, even after I was a tiny bit mean to him. And then I fell over, and I think I'm definitely probably maybe a little drunk. And I don't like it here in his arms...It feels too safe. Too familiar. Too much like I don't want to leave.

"Addie, baby, please just let me carry you a few feet so we can check on your foot."

Did he just call me baby? And was that intentional or a slip? Does he know that word makes my heart swell and break at the same time?

"Put your arms around my neck." His tone makes it clear that he will brook no further argument, and I don't offer any. I do as he asks and then he carries me back to the cabin, the scent of his cologne and the warmth of his body scrambling my senses. We don't speak again until we get inside.

"Do you want to try standing?" he asks.

My ankle is no longer throbbing and I'm sure it was just an awkward twist, so I nod.

Gently, he sets me on my feet, keeping his hands on my hips in case I fall. My ankle throbs a gentle protest, but it's fine. "I'm good."

"Yeah, you are," he says, his usually bright blue eyes incredibly dark now.

My arms are still around his neck, his hands still with a firm grip on my hips as we stare into each other's eyes. "You know I also like to wear heels because it makes me feel tall," I admit. I'm only five foot four and a lot of people are taller than me. "Except around you. Around you I always feel small."

"You're not small, Addie. I hate that I make you feel that way."

I frown, confused, and realize he's totally misunderstood my meaning. I was speaking very literally. "I only meant because you're so tall, Chase. Even in my heels you tower over me."

He grinds his jaw.

We're still holding onto each other.

"I think I kind of like that, though," I whisper, my body inching closer to his.

"Addie," he groans my name.

"What, Chase?"

"You're drunk," he says the words through clenched teeth, like he's annoyed at me for being drunk, when it's mostly his fault.

I must definitely be drunk, because I appear to have forgotten how much I hate him. "You were the one who brought me all that bourbon. I think you got me drunk on purpose."

One corner of his sinful mouth lifts in a grin. "And why exactly would I want to do that, Firefly?"

"So that I'm too hammered to stab you in your sleep, remember?"

He laughs, and the sound makes me smile too. I've always loved his laugh. Always loved...

No, Addie! No. I pull myself together and drag my

gaze away from those hypnotic eyes of his. And then I let my arms slip from around his neck. A few seconds later, he lets go of me too, and the spell is broken. "We should find you something to sleep with if you're not going to be making use of the sex swing?"

He raises an amused eyebrow. "Something to sleep with?"

"Like a blanket or something. For the couch. Not like a sex doll or anything. I didn't mean sleep with like sex; I meant actual sleeping." I mentally face-palm myself. Why would you even say that, Addie? I'm digging myself further into this hole and he keeps watching me with growing amusement.

He pinches the spot between his brows, still laughing softly. "I think we need to get you to bed."

We what now? I am not responsible for the reaction my vagina has to him uttering those words. I'm blaming the bourbon for the fact that she's screaming, *yes please, Daddy*, right now. I slip off my heels, before I fall again and take the time to re-engage my brain. "I think we've already established you're sleeping on the couch, and I will be getting myself to bed, Chase Hunter."

He holds up his hands in surrender, still smiling though. "I know, Firefly. I didn't mean..." He stops speaking. "I'm not even going there."

"No, you are not," I insist. Even though I'm not

entirely sure if he picked me up again right now and carried me to bed, I would stop him. Not sure I'd stop him if he climbed in with me. Nor if he peeled off my dress, and then my panties...

"You okay?" Chase's concerned voice pulls me from that fantasy and I realize I'm chewing on my lip and staring into space like a moron.

I nod. "Let's find you a blanket and then we can get some sleep. We have the *meet and greet* tomorrow."

"Yeah," he says, and something about the tone of his voice makes me want to wrap my arms around his neck again and just let him hold me. But again, that will be the bourbon thinking and not my brain, which knows that any display of affection would be a huge mistake.

CHAPTER 8

ADDISON

 # Who knew that making gingerbread houses is not the most exciting use for ginger?

I burrow further beneath the covers, enjoying the soft, warm duvet and the knowledge that I don't have to be anywhere but here for a while.

And then reality slaps me in the face. Chase Hunter is here. Outside this very room right now, sleeping on the sofa in my living room. So much for my peaceful few days away. Damn him messing up my alone time.

Alone time immediately makes me think of my vibrator, still tucked away in the inside pocket of my suitcase. Lonely and feeling unloved, much like me.

And while it's not an overly noisy instrument of pleasure, it's a distinctive sound, isn't it? One that can't be explained away by any other means. Can't even pretend it's my electric toothbrush, because who brushes their teeth for ten whole minutes? And I would be mortified beyond all redemption if Chase heard me getting myself off while he was in the room next door. Arrogant jerkwad would probably assume I was thinking about him and his insanely toned abs, or his cerulean-blue eyes, or maybe that smile that can melt panties at fifty paces. And I absolutely would not be thinking about any of those things, and I would definitely not be remembering how skilled he is with that mouth. It's been eight years after all. A girl doesn't still fantasize about one night eight years later!

And now I really want my vibrator. However, there's nothing to stop me from going old school and using my fingers. So, I slip my hand into my panties, circle my already swollen clit and arch my back as familiar waves of pleasure start rolling in my core. But I can't get Chase's stupid face out of my head. Can't stop remembering how good he made me feel—the kind of high I've never been able to find since, if I'm honest. However, like they always do, those good feelings inevitably lead to the bad ones—what happened after our night together, and the most intense heartbreak I've ever experienced.

Damn you to hell, Chase Hunter.

With a sigh, I jump out of bed and pull on my comfy slippers. I need some soothing ginger tea, then I can face whatever fresh hell this day has in store for me.

I have to work to suppress a snort of laughter when I leave the sanctuary of my bedroom and see Chase sleeping on the couch. He's so tall that his feet are hanging over the end. His arm is thrown over his eyes, probably to shield them from the intensely bright winter sunlight streaming through the window directly in front of him—the one we didn't close the drapes on. I try not to let my gaze linger on those incredibly toned abs he has, nor the delicious V that disappears beneath the garish purple and orange blanket we found in a closet last night, and fail abysmally. Objectively, he is a fine specimen of man candy. And I'm only looking.

"Need coffee," he groans, and I tear my eyes away and scurry to the kitchen before he finds me staring at him.

I fill the kettle and grab the box of ginger tea I brought with me before popping a teabag into a purple mug while I wait for the water to boil. When the sound of Chase's feet signal he's in the kitchen too, I don't turn around, steeling myself to not react to his incredibly muscular chest and arms. He has the kind of physique that makes a girl think about being picked up and pinned against a wall or bent over a kitchen island. Pity, his personality is so disappointing.

He begins opening and closing cupboards and he mutters curses under his breath with each one. "Where is the goddamn coffee?" he finally snaps.

I spin around and offer him a sweet smile. "I don't believe there is any."

He frowns, like I have just told him the most ridiculous thing in the history of mankind. "What kind of fucked-up, backwater place doesn't have coffee?"

"Um, the kind where you rent a cabin and have to bring your own supplies?"

He grunts, sounding like a Neanderthal, and also surprisingly hot, which I ignore. "I don't suppose you have any coffee in your box of whatever-stuff-you-grabbed-from-your-apartment-before-you-left?"

"A, how dare you assume that my box of carefully curated essentials is *stuff I grabbed from my apartment*? And, B, no, I do not."

He eyes me with suspicion and then he crosses the kitchen, heading straight for my box of random crap I totally threw in there last minute, and peers inside. "Ah, I see you prepped well for your four-day stay in an isolated cabin in the woods."

Internally, I'm wincing, but I tip my chin up and maintain my air of righteousness.

"Cheez-Its." He pulls the box out and inspects it. "That are three weeks past their use by date. Raisin bran."

"It's good for your bowels." I repeat what my mom told me when she bought me that box over six months ago. Why are you talking about bowels, Addie?

He blinks rapidly, like he wants to remove my words from his brain. "A half-empty packet of Oreos."

"Half-full, actually."

"An open packet of family-size M&M's."

"They were sealed. I opened them on the way here if you must know."

He reaches inside the box and pulls out a small packet of trail mix. "Oh, yeah. You're real prepared, Addie."

"Well, we are in the woods. Tell me where there is a more appropriate place for trail mix?"

He doesn't answer. Instead, he pulls out the box's last item. "And half a bottle of bourbon."

"Obviously."

"Tell me you didn't open that on the drive here too?"

I snatch it off him. "Of course not. Although had I known I was going to walk into the cabin and be visually assaulted by your semi-nakedness, I would have taken a good slug when I got here."

He doesn't react to my insult, maintaining his usual frustrating air of self-confidence, or self-importance. "You say semi-nakedness like I did that on purpose, but I'd just got out of the shower."

"You're semi-naked right now." I wave a hand in the general direction of his chest area. "Don't you own any shirts?"

"I just got out of bed," he protests. Then he cracks his neck and winces. "Or off of the couch—the most uncomfortable one I've ever had the displeasure of sleeping on." I feel a pang of guilt. He really did look uncomfortable on there. "And, besides, we're discussing your frankly abysmal box of *carefully curated essentials*."

"It's still a whole lot better than what you brought. Where is your contribution to our pantry, by the way?"

"I'll remind you that until two days ago, I was booked into a luxury suite at the lodge. You know that place with a restaurant. And room service. And a coffee machine," he groans while scanning the kitchen area like some finest Columbian beans may magically appear before our very eyes. And now that niggling guilt is back. Chase gave up all that comfort for me, and while it was wholly unwelcome and unnecessary, it was Brax's doing and not his. And I, of all people, know how difficult it is to resist a request from my brother. He does this sad tone and these puppy-dog eyes that make people instantly bend to his will.

I put the bourbon down and pass Chase the box of tea. "I have ginger tea too."

He pulls a disgusted face while examining the packet.

"Hey, it's better than plain old water. At least try some."

"I hate ginger," he growls.

I can't help but giggle, reminded of my college roommate and her hilarious ginger experience.

Chase scowls, obviously his lack of coffee exacerbates his already disappointing personality. "What's so funny?"

"Oh, I'm not laughing at your coffee addiction, promise. You reminded me of someone just now is all."

He discards the tea like it's offended him and then fixes me with a stare that makes goose bumps break out all over my skin, and I'm not entirely certain I don't like it. "Who did I remind you of and why?"

Okay, well now he's not so calm and composed. I guess a lack of coffee and jokes he's not in on are the things that push his buttons. I take a mental note and store it away for future reference. "Darcy, my friend from college. She hates ginger too." I snort a laugh this time, which is very inappropriate given the reason for her hatred of the delicious spice. But Darcy laughs about it now too. In fact, we laughed about it together just a few months ago.

He folds his thick forearms across his muscular chest. "Care to elaborate?"

I shouldn't, but Darcy won't care and they're never likely to meet, so why the hell not? "So, she spent a few semesters as someone's sub."

He looks even more confused. "Like a substitute teacher?"

"No, Chase. A sub, like a submissive. The guy she was with was a dom."

"Okay," he says, interest clearly piqued as he takes a seat on the stool behind him.

"She enjoyed being a bratty sub and she was really into his punishments, but this one time..." I snort another giggle, an incredibly unsexy one at that. "He punished her with ginger."

The look of absolute bewilderment on his face is almost adorable. "Ginger?"

"Don't tell me you've never heard of ginger-figging?" I ask with an exaggerated gasp. Even though I'm pretty sure I'm one of a select group of people in this world who does know what that term means.

"Ginger what-now?" Everything about him, his tone

and the look on his face is priceless, and it is deliciously satisfying to see the great Chase Hunter so perplexed.

"It's where..." I can't speak, creased with laughter now and tears rolling down my cheeks. Poor Darcy. "It's where a piece of ginger is..." I take a second to compose myself, sucking in a few deep breaths through my nose. "Inserted." I make a pushing motion with my index finger. "Somewhere that would burn. You know what I mean?"

Chase's mouth is hanging open and he's staring at me like I'm growing an extra head before his eyes.

"Chase, come on! Don't make me say it. Raw ginger would burn, right? And it was a sexual punishment. It's often coupled with spanking."

He stares at me, and then... "So, this guy shoved a piece of ginger up her ass!"

Finally, he gets it! I nod, lips pressed together, before I start laughing again.

His face is twisted in horror. "Surely, that would sting like a motherfucker?"

"Well, it's a punishment, so that's kind of the idea."

He shudders. "Why the fuck would he do that to her?"

"It was all consensual. Like I said, she was his submissive. They were actually very cute together, but after that, she couldn't even bear the smell of ginger." I clap a hand over my mouth to stop myself from laughing again.

"Fuck!" he mutters. "How long did she have to..."—he looks like he's searching for the appropriate term—"...endure the ginger for?"

"Only a little while. She said the burning didn't last more than half an hour, but while it did, it felt like she was sitting on a spike made of *fire from the devil's own secret level of hell.* And then afterward he made her feel better by..." I close my eyes and take a breath as more laughter tries to bubble its way out of me. "Let's just say it involved a snow cone and leave it there, okay?"

He nods. "Probably for the best."

"So..." I need to redirect this conversation away from BDSM punishments and the sex that inevitably follows, at least in Darcy's ginger-figging experience, and to a much safer topic. "Clearly, we need to furnish our pantry. There's a store a few miles along the highway."

He raises a brow. "You mean your carefully curated box of essentials isn't going to cut it?"

"Well, it would have been perfectly acceptable for me, but now you're here, and apparently you need coffee, so..." I shrug. I will never, not even under pain of death, admit he was right about my abhorrent lack of planning.

"Coffee, yes. And some actual food."

"Sounds good."

"And some ginger, of course. You never know when it might come in handy. Especially now I know how kinky you are." He winks and it does something to my insides that makes my legs want to wobble. And yeah, I know exactly what that's about but I'm not going to pay it any mind.

"I am not kinky," I whisper.

"You booked a cabin with a fucking sex dungeon. Do your parents know? Do Brax and Eva?"

"No, they do not and you are never going to tell them, Chase!" I tell him, mortified at the idea.

He shrugs. "I guess my silence could be bought."

Asshole! "Bought how exactly?"

He hums, head tilted to the side and now all manner of sexual favors are racing through my head. "How about you don't drive a stiletto heel through my heart this week, and I won't tell your family about your sexual proclivities. Deal?"

I swallow down my disappointment, because had he suggested buying his silence with a blow job, then I would have absolutely stabbed him through the heart with a stiletto. But the libido is a curious thing, wishing for things it has no right to wish for.

"Deal, ass-face."

"Oh, real mature, douche-nugget," he fires back.

I toss a dish towel at him and try not to laugh. And I try even harder not to think about how easy this is, just me and him. How comfortable it always was when it was just the two of us, and how we'd sometimes laugh until we couldn't breathe. He was safe and reassuring. He was a part of my life, and a part of me. It took me a long time to unlearn all of that, and just a few hours in his company are enough to have it all rushing back to me as though we've never been apart.

We had such a great thing together, and then we ruined it for one night of sex. And that's on me as much as him. But that's the unfortunate thing about mistakes, no matter how well you fix them, you can never unmake them.

CHAPTER 9
CHASE

Always name your own car, or someone else will
do it for you

Even after we unloaded all of the wedding flowers she'd managed to cram in there, Addison is still a little giddy after the whole ginger-figging revelation when we get into her ridiculous yellow car—which she has given an equally ridiculous name. And as much as the ginger thing doesn't sound like something remotely pleasurable for either party to me, I have to admit it brought up all kinds of other thoughts—specifically relating to brats and punishment, and why Addison seemed to speak about it with such...confidence. Is that what she's into now? Being punished? I mean she did book a cabin with a sex dungeon as a second bedroom for her and that douche-fuck, Jasper.

Ginger-figging isn't for me, but I could definitely get on board with a bratty Addison.

"This is it coming up, right?" She peers through the windscreen, her pathetic wipers moving at snail-like speed to clear the smattering of snow.

"No. That's a gas station. You said we're going to Kelly's Superstore, right?"

She hums to herself, turning down the radio volume as though that will somehow make it easier to see.

"We should have gotten an Uber," I grumble.

"I did tell you that you were more than welcome to. But I'm not wasting money on an Uber when I have a perfectly good car right here."

"Perfectly good is debatable," I mumble, but she hears me.

"If it wasn't below freezing outside, and Brax would never forgive me if he lost his best man to frostbite three days before his wedding, I would kick you out of my wonderful car, Chase Hunter."

She gives me my full title when she's annoyed at me, or trying to make a point, and she always has done.

"You and I have very different standards when it comes to wonderful, Addie."

"Clearly," she snorts.

I'm sure that was an insult. "What does that mean?"

"I was just agreeing with you."

"Yeah, but the way you said it, was...I don't know. Maybe you're just hardwired to give me a hard time."

"If I am, it's because you deserve it," she says and now there's a sadness to her tone that I fucking hate.

"Yeah, I do," I agree, trying to take the sting out of this conversation before it sinks us any further into our fucked-up past.

"Stop being so agreeable," she huffs.

Fuck, I can't win here, so I try a change of tactic. "Tell me why your car is named Angelina."

She takes her eyes off the road for a second and flashes me a grin. "Because she suits it, don't you think? My little Angelina." She pats the dash affectionately. "What's your car called?"

"I don't name my cars."

"Well, you should. Maybe then you'd have not wanted to leave it behind in LA and then you'd have driven here in it. Then you wouldn't be riding shotgun in mine complaining about how un-wonderful she is."

I don't point out that driving would have taken me days rather than hours, because she knows that and she's goading me. Instead, I say, "Un-wonderful isn't a word."

"I just discovered it, so it is," she says, full of defiance and sass.

I'm pretty sure I was right about the bratty side, and it makes my dick twitch very inappropriately in my jeans. "How do you know if it's a him or a her? You haven't even met it," I say, hardly even believing that I'm talking about my car like it's not simply a giant hulk of metal. It's gorgeous metal that does zero to sixty in two seconds, but it's still just metal.

"I can just tell. I'm like a car whisperer. Give me the color, make and model and I'll tell you its gender."

"It's a Bentley Continental GTC, and it's silver."

She whistles appreciatively. "Nice. And it's convertible, right?"

I'm impressed that she knows the car.

"You live in LA, of course it's a convertible," she answers her own question. "And he's definitely a he, and he should have a grand but classy name, like Faraday."

"Faraday? That's your idea of grand and classy?"

She nods, a smile spreading across her face as she keeps her eyes fixed on the road.

"Now, I'm never going to be able to look at my beautiful car ever again without calling him Faraday."

She laughs out loud and the sound makes me smile. "Aw, you called him 'him.'"

"Probably gonna have to sell him now," I grumble. "And he was custom made."

"Well, you should have named him yourself when you had the chance." She takes her eyes off the road for a second, long enough to flash me a wicked grin that does nothing to ease the situation in my jeans.

Fuck me, she has the most beautiful smile I've ever seen.

"There it is!" she yells, swerving off the highway way too fast for my comfort, not to mention Angelina's, whose brakes squeal in protest.

Addie doesn't seem to notice though and she's still smiling when we pull into the parking lot of Kelly's Superstore. "How about I drive us back?" I suggest.

"And let you loose on my precious," she says the word "precious" in her best Gollum voice, while rubbing the steering wheel and I'm reminded of how she watched all of those movies with me. When Brax and Eva declared them too long and boring, it was her who sat in her parents' den with me for an entire Sunday while we watched every one of them back-to-back. We watched them again shortly after my mom died. Just me and her.

She jumps out of the car and then quickly grabs

some tote bags from her trunk. She shoves one into my hands. "I suggest we split up. I'll grab essentials, and you get the boring stuff like food and coffee."

"Otherwise known as the things that are going to keep us alive."

She nudges me in the arm as we walk toward the entrance. "No, I said I'll be getting the essentials, you know like bourbon. And *that*, my friend, is the only thing that's gonna keep us alive."

I don't miss that she called me friend, and I don't think she does either, because her cheeks flush an adorable shade of pink.

If only to ease her growing embarrassment at admitting she doesn't hate me as much as she pretends to, I ask, "So, the plan is you get too hammered to be able to wield a knife and kill me in my sleep?"

She nods. "Exactly."

"Sounds as good a plan as any, I guess."

She claps me on the shoulder, and the contact has my skin warm, even through my sweater and coat. "It's the only way, Chase."

She spins in the opposite direction and I watch her dark head disappearing as she turns down one of the aisles. And then I take a second to breathe and remind myself that I'm only doing this as a favor to Brax. I'm here for four more days and just because Addie is tolerating me, doesn't mean we're miraculously going to rekindle our old friendship, and definitely not anything more.

So, stop looking at her and thinking all of the things you're thinking about doing, Chase! She's not yours anymore. You had her and you fucked it up! Asshole.

With that thought in my head, I wander in the direction of the grocery aisle to find some food and coffee.

BY THE TIME Addie and I meet up again at the register, I have an entire shopping cart laden with food and other essentials, such as toilet paper. She casts an eye over my choices and grudgingly gives her approval. I glance in her basket, filled with cookies, chips, candy, a bottle of Buffalo Trace—her favorite bourbon—and nestled against it is a bottle of Woodford Reserve—mine. I know her favorite bourbon because I low-key stalk her social media, which is incredibly lacking in any kind of regard for her personal safety or security, but she's actually remembered mine.

I grind my jaw to stop myself from smiling at that, and she helps me unload my cart. When that's done, I grab the items from her basket and add them to mine.

"Good idea. We can just split it fifty-fifty."

I shake my head. "This is on me."

"Nuh-uh. I pay for my own stuff. I don't need your—"

"Addie!" I don't mean to say her name like that, like a command, but I don't miss the way her hazel eyes darken at my tone, nor the way she immediately gives me her undivided attention. "You paid for the entire cabin, and I know I wasn't your intended roommate, but I want to pay my way. Please just let me do this, okay?"

She stares at me, her chin tilted and her jaw working. "No way. You might be invading my cabin this week, but let's get one thing straight, you are less guest and more unwelcome intruder. And you do not get to assuage your guilty conscience for ruining my wonderful, idyllic getaway by bribing me with pasta and toilet paper. Capisce?"

I want to argue. Fuck, I want to toss her over my shoulder, march her outside and kiss that sassy mouth until she stops yelling at me. But I absolutely cannot do any of that.

So, I relent. "Fine."

"Fine," she parrots.

Brat!

~

STILL BEING as stubborn as a mule, Addie refuses to let me drive her precious Angelina back to the cabin. And infuriatingly, she insists on listening to her own *carefully curated* playlist on the way back, a playlist which consists of annoying, cheesy Christmas songs. It's not that I'm some kind of monster who hates Christmas; it's just that it's historically not been the happiest time of my life. At least as an adult. My mom always did what she could to make the holidays special. She was a waitress in a diner and our Christmases usually involved me sitting with some coloring books and waiting for her to finish her shift. It was still fun though. We'd take leftovers home and watch Christmas movies while stuffing our faces with turkey, and then cheesecakes for dessert. Then, she died a few weeks before Christmas while I was in my last year of college. So that holiday sucked ass. And then the following one...well, that was the year Addie and I hooked up.

"I love this song!" She turns up the volume super loud and begins singing along. Addison Kinsella is a woman of many talents, but singing is not one of them. I suppress a smile at her off-key vocals. But then the lyrics hit me, and now I'm overwhelmed with memories of that night.

I doubt she even realizes the significance of this song, but I watched her dancing to "Santa Tell Me" at

Hugo Pierson's Christmas party. I still recall what she was wearing in technicolor detail even now: blue skinny jeans, a tight, red sweater with the words "I'm on Santa's Naughty List" written across the front and pair of sky-high red Louboutins that her parents had bought her for her eighteenth birthday—her pride and joy.

And fuck but the way she danced, like she didn't care who was watching her, even though I know for sure I wasn't the only guy staring at her and drooling over the way her hips moved so perfectly to the music. Her confidence was sexy as fuck, and all the times I'd told myself I shouldn't look at her that way because she was my best friend's sister seemed to melt into nothing. And then she smiled at me, right as she was singing the part about "getting on top of him by that fireplace" and I was done for.

I took her home and even though we kissed in the park, and then again on her porch, I still tried to convince myself that nothing more would happen. Except it did. We shared something incredible.

And then I fucked it all to hell.

CHAPTER 10
ADDISON
EIGHT YEARS AGO

I can't believe this is actually happening. My mouth is dry. My heart beating erratically in my chest. How did we even get here? We were at a party, and I was dancing, and I was sure Chase was watching me but assumed I was delusional because he's, well, he's Chase Hunter—former star quarterback, my brother's best friend and three years older than me. Then Chase's friend, Freddie, got way too drunk and was being an asshole, and Chase asked if I wanted to leave, and of course I said yes.

We were walking through the park and talking about how much he missed his mom, and I told him how we all miss Karen too. Then I hugged him, and he kissed me. And my soul left my body because I have never wanted to be kissed by anyone quite as much as

I've wanted to be kissed by him. And it was everything I dreamed it would be and more. He's so confident and assured. So skilled with his mouth and tongue.

And now we're lying on my bed, and he's kissing my neck and moaning my name, and my panties are soaked, and he's barely even touched me yet. I run my fingers through his thick, dark hair, grinding my hips against him.

"You're so fucking sexy, Addie," he groans, sounding pained. "Are you sure you want to do this?"

I nod, lip caught between my teeth. I've never wanted anything more.

He growls. "You have no fucking idea how long I've waited to taste you, baby."

He's been waiting...for me? My head spins faster. I'm certain this must be a dream. He kisses my neck again and then he's moving lower, his hands pushing up my sweater until his lips are on my stomach. And then he's unbuttoning my jeans.

Oh, dear, sweet baby Jesus. "Chase!" I gasp, my entire body trembling with nervous excitement.

He stops, his deep blue eyes fixed on mine. "What is it, Firefly?"

I blush at the nickname, the one he's called me since I was eight years old and he found me catching light-ning bugs. "I—I've never done this before," I admit.

He blinks and now I feel foolish. It's not like I haven't had plenty of opportunities to; I've just never really wanted to take that next step. Probably because I compare every guy I ever date to the one currently lying on top of me, and not a single one makes my entire body come alive the way that he does. "You've never had sex?"

I shake my head.

"Fuck, Addie," he says, and I can't tell if he's annoyed or feeling sorry for me, or confused, or all three.

"I'm not a prude or anything, I've just—"

He seals his lips briefly over mine, stopping my nervous babbling. "I never for a second thought you were, and it's okay. We don't have to do anything more than this if you like." He licks across the seam of my lips, and I part them on a gasp before he slips his tongue into my mouth and kisses me so deeply, he almost takes my breath away. When he pulls back, he offers me a wicked grin. "I fucking love kissing you."

I glide my hands over his back, reveling in the feeling of his hard muscles beneath his shirt. "I want to do this, Chase. I want to do this with you."

He stares into my eyes. "You don't have to."

"I know that. But I really really want to."

His eyes rake over my face and his blue eyes grow

dark with undisguised hunger. "You've really never had sex?"

I shake my head.

He drags his teeth gently along my jawline. "So, just how far have you gone before, Addie?"

"Third base. With a couple of guys..." I feel embarrassed talking about that with him. Even though I dated both of them, I never wanted to go any further. It was never quite...this.

Chase hums softly, trailing his lips over my jaw. "And did they make you come?"

My entire body flushes with heat at his words. "No," I whisper. I always thought I'd feel self-conscious for my first time, but I don't with him. "I've made myself come though. Lots of times." Mostly while imagining it was you touching me. I keep that latter thought to myself.

He groans softly, warm breath dancing over my skin and making goose bumps prickle out over my flesh. "Good girl," he murmurs and his words travel straight to my core.

I slide my hand to the zipper of his jeans and he grunts when I pull it down. "Not yet, Firefly. Let me make sure you're ready first."

I'm more than ready? Doesn't he realize I've been waiting for this moment for years? Waiting for him. "I'm ready, Chase," I whine.

He tuts, pinning my hands on either side of my head. "I love how much you want this, Addie, but I'll decide when you're ready."

Chase undresses me torturously slowly, his hands and mouth exploring every single inch of me—all except for the space between my thighs that's aching for his touch. "You're even more beautiful than I imagined, Firefly," he growls.

When he sucks one of my pebbled nipples into his mouth, a lightning bolt of pleasure shoots right through me and I whimper with need. "Chase, please!"

"It's okay, baby," he says, soft and soothing. "I've got you."

Then his hand slides between my legs and already I feel like I might pass out. He rubs gentle circles over my clit and my core contracts. And then his fingers move closer to my entrance. When he pushes a thick finger inside me, my back bows and I coat him in a rush of arousal.

"Fuck, you're soaked, Addie," he says through clenched teeth. "My naughty fucking girl."

He plants one powerful forearm beside my head, a wall of sinew and muscle, and holds himself up while he expertly slides his finger in and out of me. When he adds a second, I'm hit with an overwhelming rush of euphoria. I know this act is colloquially known as fingerbanging, and I'd have wholeheartedly agreed with that term in the past, but nothing about what Chase is doing could be described as that at all. He is skilled and experienced, every move he makes precise and powerful, yet tender and reverent.

His mouth brushes over mine. "You're doing so good for me."

"Yeah?"

He kisses me, soft yet possessive. "Uh-huh. Your tight little pussy is squeezing my fingers so hard. Desperate to come."

Pleasure is building in my core, snaking through my limbs and winding through my veins. He's staring down at me, his eyes intense and his mouth twitching with the hint of a smile while he watches me unravel beneath him.

"You look so fucking beautiful coming undone for me, Firefly."

I suck in a stuttered breath. Light flickers behind my eyelids. He sinks his fingers deeper and brushes the pad of his thumb over my clit and I explode like a billion tiny fire bursts.

His mouth rests against my ear. "There she is," he says softly, gently working his fingers to coax every ounce of ecstasy from my trembling body. I'm still shaking when he slides his fingers out of me. He holds my gaze when he places them in his mouth and sucks them clean, humming appreciatively. When he releases them, he curses under his breath.

"Is everything okay?"

"No." He grins at me. "You taste incredible, and I think you're about to ruin me for any other woman, Addie Kinsella."

He brushes my hair back from my face and holds my chin gently in his hands. "And I really want to eat your pussy and make you come on my face, but I think I might nut in my jeans if I did. And I think my little Firefly really needs fucking first, so..."

I can't suppress the wide smile that spreads across my face. I have never in my life before been this happy. "I'm on birth control," I assure him.

For some reason that makes him bite on his lip and groan, "I've never ever fucked a girl without a condom, Addie."

"So that means it would be safe for us not to use one?"

His blue eyes flash dark with hunger. "Only if you're okay with that. I have one in my jacket. I can go get it right now."

I also know where Brax keeps a stash, but I don't tell him that. Because I want to feel nothing between us for my first time. "No, I want to feel all of you."

"You're sure?"

I nod. "I would also like to see all of you."

He arches an eyebrow. "I guess that's only fair."

He jumps off the bed and tugs his shirt over his head, revealing his incredible physique. I try not to drool, because it's not like I haven't seen it before, at least his top half anyway, but this still feels different. Then he kicks off his sneakers and socks and unbuttons his jeans. When he slides them over his hips, along with his black boxers, I can't help myself from gasping aloud at the sight of him. I've seen guys before, even held a few of their dicks in my hands, but none have been as thick as Chase's. It stands proudly, its purple crown beaded with a white pearl of precum.

I swallow my nerves and let my excitement take over again. Once he's naked, he crawls over me. "There's no need to be nervous, Firefly. We can take this as slow as you want to, okay?"

"Okay," I pant.

My pulse flutters against my neck like a butterfly's wings, and he flicks his tongue over it as he spreads my thighs apart with his knees, until the thick head of him is nudging at my entrance. "It might hurt a little at first, but then as soon as I'm inside you, it will be okay. If you need me to stop at any point, you just tell me, understand?"

I suck in a shuddering breath. "Yes."

He inches the tip inside me and it feels so good that I cry out. "You have no idea how many times I've thought about this," he growls. "And you feel even better than I thought you would."

"I've thought about it too," I admit, floored by his revelation, but too caught up in this moment to unpack what it means.

He looks down at the place where our bodies are joined and groans, "Fuck, Addie, I wish you could see how good you look with my cock stretching you open."

I look down, but all I see is him holding back from sinking inside me, his muscles vibrating with the sheer effort of his restraint. I do feel stretched, but it's such a delicious kind of ache and I want so much more. "Just do it, Chase. I want all of you," I whine.

He braces himself, hands planted either side of my head. And then he sinks all the way inside me, and it does hurt a little, like he said it would, but in a way that feels so damn good. My body lights up from the inside, liquid heat burning in my veins.

"That's my good girl. You're taking me so fucking well," Chase says, the deep timber of his voice soothing and igniting at the same time.

I wrap my arms around his neck, clinging to him as he pulls out and sinks all the way back inside me again. "My cock feels so good filling your pussy, Addie. So fucking good. You're squeezing me so tight."

I throw my head back, sinking into the soft pillow. "Don't stop. Please don't ever stop!"

His teeth graze over my neck. "I'm not gonna stop, baby. Not ever. This pussy is mine now, you got that. Mine."

He sinks even deeper, hitting a spot inside me that makes my eyes roll back. "Oh, fuck, Chase."

"I know. You're gonna come on my cock this time."

I am. I can't stop. Can't hold back the torrent of ecstasy that's washing over every part of me. Now I know why I waited so long to have sex. I was waiting for this. For him.

I WAKE up with his arms still wrapped around me and his chest pressed up against my back. Every single muscle in my body aches, but in that delicious way like after an intense workout. I smile and wiggle my ass against him.

He nips my shoulder. "Are you looking to be fucked again, Addie?" he murmurs.

I giggle, recalling how I woke him in the night to

have sex again, and how happy he was to oblige. "No. Just enjoying lying here."

"Does Santa know what a naughty girl you are?"

"You said I was a good girl last night," I remind him.

"Hmm. You were a very good girl." He trails kisses over my neck.

"Brax and my parents will be home soon," I say, even though I know it's going to break this wonderful moment.

"Ugh," he groans. "Then I guess I'd better leave."

I swallow down my disappointment. But he places his pointer finger under my chin and tilts my head until I'm looking at him. "I have some things to take care of, but then I'll see you tonight and we'll talk. Okay?"

"Okay."

He drops a kiss on my nose. "That's my good girl."

He jumps out of bed and I watch him dress, letting my eyes rake over his toned, muscular body. Chase has never been short of girlfriends and maybe I'm being foolish to think he will ever want more than a casual hookup with me, but last night, he said all those things. About me being his and how I was about to ruin him for any other woman. Still, I'm not naïve enough to think that those kinds of things can't be said in the heat of the moment.

He sits on the edge of my bed when he's fully dressed. "What is it, Firefly?"

I screw my eyes closed. "I know I'm Brax's sister and we have a whole history. I—I just don't want things to be awkward between us. I know I'm inexperienced but I'm not naïve, Chase." I stop short of telling him that it would be okay if this was a casual hookup, because it wouldn't be. But I also don't want to sound desperate.

He cups my jaw and leans in for a brief kiss. "I know you're not, Addie. We'll talk later. Okay?"

Even the tone of his voice has a kaleidoscope of butterflies taking flight in the pit of my stomach. "Okay."

He kisses me again. "I'll see you tonight."

He walks out of my room and leaves me lying in bed, a stupid, goofy grin on my face, a full heart and a delicious ache between my thighs. Although I always knew it, now I am one hundred percent certain that I'm undeniably and irrefutably in love with Chase Hunter, and I'm going to be in love with him for the rest of my life.

CHAPTER II

CHASE

 # Never keep secrets from a woman capable of stabbing you through the heart with a stiletto

After Addie and I unloaded Angelina, we walked to the main lodge to meet up with the wedding party, although not until I questioned once again the appropriateness of her choice of footwear. I swear she's wearing those heels to drive me crazy.

Today is all about *getting to know each other*. Despite Eva growing up in Juniper Ridge with her mom, most of her family live across the world and she doesn't get to see them often. When her mom married her stepdad, Josh, she got another new family. And much like the Kinsella family get togethers, most of *getting to know each other* is based around the eating of food. There's afternoon tea, because Eva's mom, Helen, is British and apparently that's a thing there, and then a sit-down dinner later. Now that Addie and I have our truce, I'm sure today will be much more fun than yesterday. I would never tell her parents or her brother she's a sexual deviant, but she doesn't need to know that.

I open the door for her and she offers me a smile, one so sweet that it's obviously fake.

Brax practically tackles her to the floor as soon as we get into the lobby. "Addie. Please tell me you're not still mad at me for the whole cabin misunderstanding," he pleads.

I catch her eye and grin, reminding her of our truce too. "Of course I'm not, Brax," she says, and actually, I'm sure she's not mad at him. Not only is he impossible to stay mad at, but she's also aware that it's not his fault he doesn't know what a bad idea us sharing a cabin is. That's all on us.

Brax is soon pulled away by a distant relative, of either his or Eva's, but he's replaced by his dad, Jack.

"Hi, sweetheart," he says to Addie, wrapping his

arm around her. She's the apple of his eye and I love their relationship. My dad died when I was seven, and since I've known Jack, he has always been like a father to me. His relationship with Addie is the kind of one I'd like to have if I ever have a daughter. "Your aunt Irene keeps asking me if you need any help putting the table decorations together tomorrow, but don't worry, I told her you had it all in hand." He winks, conspiratorially.

She smiles. "Thanks, Dad."

"If you do need any actual help, I'm sure Chase here would be more than happy to lend a hand."

I nod. "Sure. More than happy to."

The smile she gives me is tight and forced. "I'm sure I can handle it on my own."

Jack kisses her forehead. "I know you can. You're incredible at what you do. And I'm so proud of you, sweetheart. You saw what you wanted and you went for it. You turned that old flower store around and made it the successful business it is today." Then he turns his attention to me. Fuck! I think I know what he's about to say and I give him a subtle shake of my head, but it's too late. "You sure made a good investment there, son." He nudges me in the arm.

Addie blinks at the two of us in confusion. Of course she does because she has no idea what I have to do with her store, on account of me swearing Jack and Maggie to secrecy. Way to throw me under the bus, Jack! "What do you mean, Dad?" she asks innocently.

Immediately realizing his error, Jack Kinsella mumbles something about needing another Scotch and then he practically runs to the bar, leaving me to clean up the can of worms he just opened. Great!

"What did he mean, Chase? Why would he say that about my store?"

I take a breath and hope for the best. There's no easy way to tell her this, so I simply rip off the Band-Aid and blurt it out. "I own your store, Addie."

She blinks. Once. Twice. "You what now?"

"I own your store."

"I know that's what you said, but what? How? Why?" Each question gets progressively louder and I steer her away to a less crowded part of the lobby. She plants her hands on her hips. "You'd better start talking, Chase Hunter."

Again with the full title. "It's not that complicated, Addie. The guy who owned your store and the other half dozen around it was selling up. Some sportswear giant was looking at it for some superstore, so I bought it to stop that from happening. It's not a big deal."

"It's a big deal to me. You *own* my store, Chase! How could you not tell me that? Does everyone know?"

I shake my head. "Only your mom and dad, and I asked them to keep it between us."

She folds her arms across her chest and it makes her already distracting cleavage even more apparent. I work to keep my eyes on her face, because I'm not a sleaze and I don't look at women's boobs when I'm talking to them as a rule, but I happen to know what these ones feel like, taste like...

"What the hell, Chase? How dare you keep that a secret from me?"

"And this is exactly why I did, Addie. You're so pissed there's practically steam coming out of your ears."

"Because you and my parents lied to me."

"We did not lie...we merely didn't disclose all of the facts. And why am I the only one getting reamed for it?"

"Because"—she jabs a finger in my chest—"I am one hundred percent certain that it was your idea to keep it from me. Am I right?"

"Technically, yes. But be honest, Addie, what would you have done if you'd found out it was me buying those stores? You'd have closed up and moved to another part of town just to avoid having anything to do with me, wouldn't you?"

She at least has the good grace not to lie to my face and deny that, because we both know it's true. Instead, she covers her eyes and sighs. "Why on earth did you do that, Chase?"

"It was a good business decision. Those stores on your block are prime real estate."

Her hand drops from her face and her eyes widen in surprise. "You own them all?"

I nod.

She's still glaring at me. "You could have bought real estate anywhere. Why Juniper Ridge?"

"Because it's my home, Addie. I care about the town, and the people in it. But if you want the honest truth, mostly, I did it for the same reason I helped Brax out with his repair shop." I shouldn't have admitted that last part, should have kept it all about business, but she gets under my skin so damn easily.

"But that's because he's your best friend."

"No, he's my family, Addison."

I can see her wrestling with what I just said and practically hear her arguing with herself in her own head, because there was a time when she considered me her family too.

"I might have fucked up our friendship, and anything else we were ever going to be, Addie, but you will always be my family, and I would do anything for you, just like I would for Brax."

She wants to argue with me, I can see it in her face,

but beneath all of that fire and sass, she's also one of the most compassionate people I know. And she of all people knows how hard it is for me to admit that, to be vulnerable with anyone. Her slender neck works as she swallows. "I don't like being kept in the dark about things pertaining to my own life, Chase. You should have told me."

I hold my hands up in surrender. "I fully agree and I intended to, but the timing never seemed to be quite right."

Her brows pinch in a frown. "Hold up. I thought my building was owned by a guy named Brian from Idaho? I speak to him like once a month. So, who the hell is he?"

Shit! He is the reason I know almost everything about your life. "He's one of my project managers."

"Your project manager? I've been speaking to one of your project managers for the past four years? I know the names of his wife and children. I talk to him about all kinds of stuff, Chase."

Yeah, I know! "That's not exactly my fault you two hit it off so well, though."

Her cheeks are growing pinker with each passing second. With indignation or embarrassment, I can't yet tell, possibly both. "Does he tell you what we talk about?"

Internally I'm wincing hard, but I maintain at least an air of outward composure. Yes. Yes, he fucking does. It's how I know about every disastrous relationship you've had for the past four years and the reason you drink pink wine. I should be ashamed of myself, but I'm really not. "I'm sure he doesn't tell me *everything*."

"Wow, Chase. You're a real piece of work."

She storms off in a huff, moving faster than any person should be able to in those heels. I go after her, having to jog to reach her. And then, before I know it, I have my hand on her arm and I'm pulling her into one of the lobby's many dark little alcoves. "Addie, please just fucking listen to me."

She wrenches her arm free and then tips her jaw up, glaring at me. "I'm all ears."

"I am sorry that I didn't *tell you* I bought your store, but I am not even a little sorry that I did. And I am definitely not sorry that I had one of my most trusted employees be the man who overlooks the running of those properties. I get that you feel blindsided. I get that you don't want to be sharing a cabin, or probably even a continent with me, but we are. And we're in this wedding party, and this constant friction is exhausting. Can we please just pretend that we're not mortal enemies? For a few days? For Brax and Eva?"

Her eyes narrow on mine. She looks like she might

explode like a tiny little volcano of rage and sass, and yet I can't stop imagining pinning her against this wall and kissing her so hard neither of us will remember what the hell we were arguing about. "What did you mean before when you said you fucked up anything else we were ever going to be?"

And now I'm blindsided. "What?"

"You said you were sorry you fucked up our friendship and whatever else we might have been. What else might we have been, Chase?"

Shitting fuck! What new level of hell are we entering here? If she was intending to turn the tables and have me on the back foot then she has totally succeeded. How do I even answer that? You *might* have been the only woman I've ever loved and we *might* have been married with four kids by now? "I don't know what I was...I was just making a point, Addie."

She edges closer, and instinctually I do too, and now there's only a few inches between us. Her eyes are dark, still glowing with anger, but maybe something else lingers there now too. My pulse is racing. Her breathing gets shallower. We both lean in and her tits brush against my chest. Do not look down at them right now, Chase! My dick is already at DEFCON 2 and it would take nothing more than the hint of a smile from her lips to make him harder than iron.

Her lips part and I am seconds away from kissing them. There's nothing in this entire world right now but her and me and this moment. No past. No future...

"Addie, darling," Maggie's voice slices through the tension like a surgeon's blade. Addie's eyes immediately leave mine and land on her mom. An intense wave of frustration washes over me, but I take a much-needed breath and then I twist around too. "Your father should never have mentioned anything about Chase buying up those storefronts. I swear give him a little whiskey and he folds faster than a wet newspaper." She shakes her head.

"It's okay, Maggie..." I start, but she shushes me.

"It was none of his business saying that to you, and you, my girl, don't you dare be giving Chase a hard time when all he was doing was helping out." Her tone is all business, but there's no real bite to it. Maggie Kinsella adores her kids, and if she knew how I'd broken her daughter's heart, she wouldn't just *threaten* to stab me with a stiletto. I'd be six feet under right now.

"She wasn't giving me a hard time, Maggie. I swear."

Maggie' eyes narrow on Addie like she doesn't quite believe me. Unsurprisingly, given how well she knows her daughter. Addison is a firecracker because she was raised by one.

Addie flashes me a brief scowl. "I think I'm perfectly entitled to know who my landlord is, Mom."

Maggie considers that for a second and then nods. "Well, yes, you are. But Chase simply didn't want anyone to know. He was just doing a good deed." She smiles at me like I'm a fucking hero or something, and I can feel the heat from Addie's fierce glare on my skin. I'm sure she's thinking that I'm less white knight and more heartless villain, and I wonder if she regrets not telling her family what an asshole I was to her. I'm eternally grateful that she didn't but I hate that it puts her in these awkward situations.

"There you all fucking are. What the fuck is going on?" Brax says and I try not to groan out loud at his arrival. If they'd just given me one more minute...then what? They'd have found me with my hands on Addison's ass and my tongue down her throat. Probably better they did interrupt us actually.

"Braxton Benjamin Kinsella," Maggie chides. "Must you use that word so liberally?" She shakes her head at him.

He throws his hands up. "It's just a fucking word, Mom."

She links her arm through mine and tuts. "He uses fuck like a comma that boy. Now, let's all get to our afternoon tea, shall we? And there'll be no more nonsense from any of you."

Brax rolls his eyes at me and then he drapes an arm around his sister. He whispers something to her that makes her giggle, but I'm already escorting—or being escorted by—Maggie back to the banquet hall. And now whatever moment we were just sharing is long gone, but I have three more days and nights to get it back.

CHAPTER 12

ADDISON

Drinking bourbon-laced tea in front of a roaring log fire is not foreplay

T still can't stop thinking about what Chase said earlier today even though I really should. *I fucked up our friendship, and anything else we were ever going to be.* What the hell did he even mean by that? Jackass is messing with my head.

I was just a hookup to him. Someone he felt sorry for. Someone he *threw a bone.* I don't let myself get too caught up in that memory because it's too painful, and also, after our incredibly intense encounter today in the lobby, we managed to have a pleasant afternoon. More than pleasant actually. Chase made Eva's mom snort laugh with some of his stories from when they were kids—he's always been great at making people smile. After the afternoon tea was over, we all hung around the lobby until dinner. It was a truly special day, full of family and friends and laughter.

And afterward Chase and I walked back to the cabin and I changed into my pajamas while he made us some tea—ginger for me and rooibos for him—and he lit the fire too, the one we're currently sitting in front of. Me on a beanbag and him on the sofa, and a bottle of bourbon on the table between us.

Chase pours a generous slug into his tea and then offers me the same, and of course I gratefully accept, because the only thing cozier than tea by a roaring fire is bourbon in said tea.

"So, tell me again how Brian came to be my landlord?" I ask.

He winces, screwing up his eyes and muttering a string of curses before he answers. And I'm glad he feels bad about it. He damn well should. "I knew you'd be pissed if you thought it was me, and I also knew those units needed an overhaul. So, I put my best project manager on the job to get it all handled as quickly and professionally as possible."

I sip my tea and mull that over. It is true that shortly

after Brian became my landlord, we did get new plumbing and electrics, not to mention new energy-efficient storefront windows. Chase's company is big on green energy and it's one of the things I've always grudgingly admired about his business.

"And the monthly calls?"

He smirks. "Well, he calls all of his tenants, but I admit you're the only one he ever told me he stayed on a call with for more than two minutes."

I can feel my cheeks flushing. A few hours after the very first time I spoke to him, his four-year-old son, Oscar, called me; I assumed Brian had left his phone unlocked and the kid had been playing around. Oscar and I had a lovely chat before his dad took the phone and apologized. I told him it was no big deal and then we talked about his kids and his wife, and I ended up telling him about my disastrous date the night before, and that was the start of a beautiful friendship...or so I thought. "Does he tell you what we talk about?"

Chase takes a healthy slug of his tea. "I will admit I do show more interest in you than any of the other tenants, but only because you're..." His blue eyes narrow on my face and I feel like wriggling in my seat under the intense scrutiny of his gaze, but I don't. Chase looking at me like that also makes me feel like wriggling in my seat for an entirely different reason. "Well, you're you."

"Who else would I be, Chase?"

He smiles, that lazy, lopsided grin that used to, and unfortunately still does, make him look far too sexy for his own good.

Recalling the many conversations I've had with Brian about my disastrous relationships, I ask, "Does he keep you up to speed on my dating life too?"

"I mean he doesn't give me details," he says, a sheepish grin on his face.

"Wow!" I shake my head. "Brian is a sneak."

"He's just doing his job, and he really likes you. Don't be mad at the guy. I showed an interest in you and I'm his boss so...But Jasper though? Really?" He tilts his head to the side and the twinkle in his eyes is far too playful and mischievous. It should be a siren telling me to run far and fast from this conversation. But it's comfy here in front of the fire, so I don't.

"You don't even know him."

"I know he's a douche-knuckle."

I scoff. "How?"

"Because he dumped you." He flashes me a wicked grin while he tops up my ginger tea with a generous slug of bourbon.

"You think you're so smooth, Chase Hunter. But like I said, you don't even know him. So don't judge me."

He raises an amused eyebrow. "You mean the *micro-brewer with the heart of a lion?*"

I snort a laugh that has ginger tea coming out of my nose, but I'm too busy giggling to care. I wipe my face with the sleeve of my sweater. "You've seen his Instagram page?"

He nods. "Top-notch douche-knuckle."

"Well, he at least had the hair of a lion," I say through my laughter. "Honestly, I'm sure I'll still be finding strands of his long, blond hair in my drain when I'm a grandma."

Chase shifts forward in his seat, blue eyes laser focused on my face. "A grandma, huh?"

"What? Is that unusual?"

He shakes his head. "So, you want the whole marriage and kids thing?"

Oh, wow, this conversation took a turn, but I deflect like a pro. "Why have you seen my ex-boyfriend's Instagram?"

He shrugs. "Eva told me you were cut up about him, so I checked him out."

I sigh and roll my eyes. "I wasn't cut up about him."

"One of these days, Addie, I'm going to spank your ass when you roll those pretty eyes at me." He takes a swig of his tea like he didn't just say something wildly inappropriate, and also something which has images of him spanking me now burned into my brain. "So, you were just cut up about attending this wedding solo?" he goes on.

I blink at him. How the hell does he know that? And if I admit that, then I admit that I was worried about having to see his douchey face in person. "No," I insist. "Maybe I was upset about Jasper," I lie with ease. "So, sue me."

His jaw works, making him appear annoyed. He takes a big gulp of his tea before topping up his mug and when he looks at me again, his eyes are softer. "So that was just me worried about attending this wedding solo then?"

"You were cut up about having to attend Brax and Eva's wedding on your own?"

He hums to himself. "Not cut up, no. But I did wonder about bringing a date. If only to stop all the questions, or the pitying looks."

"People definitely pity women more than men at these kinds of things," I remind him. "Single men are carefree bachelors, while women are reminded of their *biological clocks.*"

He nods, like he agrees with that assessment.

Damn, why is he so charming and easy to talk to, and why am I so desperate to know more about his personal life? I've been able to glean enough about him from Brax and Eva over the years. He dates. *A lot!* But he's never had a serious relationship, at least none that he's told them about anyway. "So, why didn't you? Bring a date I mean?"

"Inviting someone to a wedding is a pretty huge step. Especially bringing them to Brax and Eva's wedding. It's basically introducing someone to my family."

"And there's nobody who you want to take that step with?" I ask, probing more than I should, but this is just a conversation between...well, two people who used to be friends at least.

He shakes his head. "You obviously did though. With Jasper. The guy you booked a cabin with that has a sex dungeon?" There's an edge to his voice now that makes him sound a little annoyed.

I roll my eyes. "That was not the reason I booked this cabin," I insist.

His eyes narrow and I'm reminded of that eye-roll comment he made, and how it does things to my insides that are both unwelcome and yet delicious. But he doesn't make good on his threat to spank me, fortunately—or not. "So, you weren't planning on a four-night fuck-a-thon with your heart-of-a-lion boyfriend?"

Another snort of laughter, although this time minus the ginger tea being forcefully ejected from my nose. I shake my head. "Definitely not any kind of fuck-a-thon." I internally shudder at the thought. "I suppose I did want to stop all the awkward 'Are you still single?' questions though."

"You do want to get married though? Have kids? Become a grandma?"

And now we're back here again. "You don't need to be married to have kids, you know?"

He grins. "I know. Stop dodging the question."

Do I give him honesty? Does he deserve it? I take another sip of my bourbon-infused tea before I answer. "Yeah, I do. When I left college, I had these big dreams about seeing the world and becoming someone extraordinary. And then I saw the world, and you know what?"

He's staring at me intently. Listening. It feels like forever since a guy has actually listened to me, while not trying to get into my pants. "What?" His voice is deep and sensual even when he doesn't intend it to be.

"I loved my time abroad. I had experiences that I'll remember for the rest of my life, but the entire time I was away, I really missed home. And I realized that what I really wanted for my life wasn't even close to the dreams I'd convinced myself I should have. In fact, they were a hell of a lot smaller. Not all that extraordinary after all."

His bright blue eyes are still fixed on my face. "I don't think any dreams are small, Addie, if they're what we truly want."

I suppose he has a point there. Damn eloquent asshole. "I guess. Although the house I want to live in with my adoring husband and our darling children, who will be the perfect blend of both of us, isn't small."

He grins. "No? And which house would that be?"

"The old Cooper Place on Hope Street. You know the one with the wraparound porch and the swing. It's been up for sale for almost a year now and I can't believe nobody has snapped it up."

"I remember the place. Brax and I used to steal the peaches from their trees out back."

"You have real light fingers when it comes to fruit, don't you?" I tease him.

He shrugs. "There are worse flaws to have than being a fruit thief, I guess."

Yeah, like stealing hearts. I don't say that though, and he didn't exactly steal my heart, or my virginity. I gave them both willingly.

"So, you don't plan on leaving Juniper Ridge again?" he asks.

I shake my head. "I don't think so. I feel right there, you know? Like it's where I'm supposed to be. Not extraordinary. Just me."

"I think you're pretty extraordinary, Addison Kinsella." He pours a little more bourbon into his tea.

Is he just saying that to make me feel better, or does he mean it? "I think you're pretty extraordinary too, Chase Hunter," I admit, and then immediately feel vulnerable for having done so. "But then you always were. Star athlete. Homecoming King. Hotshot, award-winning architect."

He takes a swig of his tea, which is now probably just bourbon and not tea at all. "They're just things I've done. I don't think they're the kinds of things that make people extraordinary."

"Then what does?" I ask, aware of the tremor in my voice.

"The ability to make the people around you feel something, I guess. Loved. Happy. Cared for. Protected. Kindness is underrated, especially in LA." He clears his throat. "So, tell me more about this new dream of yours."

"When I was younger, I always thought marriage and kids were the easy choice, you know? The thing I could do if my fantasies of traveling the world didn't work out. But now sometimes it feels like that's the dream that's farthest away. I look at my mom and dad and see how happy they are, and I guess I always assumed that I'd find that one day too. But, I don't know, I think I'm running out of options."

He rolls his eyes. Maybe I should threaten to spank his ass. "You're twenty-seven."

"I said options, not time, dumbass." I throw a cushion at his head, but he catches it with ease.

He sticks the cushion behind his back. "Why on earth do you think that?"

I sigh. "I love my store. I love my family and my friends and..." I search for the right words. "Our town is so small, I feel like everyone has already found their someone, you know? And all the people who are left are left for a reason...like me." I force out a laugh, so I don't cry and sink the last of my ginger-bourbon tea. "Or are passing through, like Jasper."

He stares at me, like he's going to speak, but he doesn't.

I voice the fear I haven't wanted to admit to myself for a while now. "I sometimes wonder if there's only one person for everyone, then how will I find mine in Juniper Ridge?"

CHAPTER 13

CHASE

 # Never confuse your Bart Simpson with your Götz von Berlichingen

I stare at the ceiling, listening to the soft crackling of the fire and replaying her words over and over.

I sometimes wonder if there's only one person for everyone, then how will I find mine in Juniper Ridge?

It took everything in me not to ask her what if she'd already found them?

Because I did leave Juniper Ridge, and I've still never found anyone who even comes close to her. Not a single person who challenges me the way that she does, or who makes me want to be a better man. No one with a kinder heart or a purer soul, who looks at me like I'm the person they've been waiting for their whole life. Nobody who moans my name quite the same way that she does.

And as wrong as it is, I can't stop wondering what might happen if I went into her room and reminded her how good we could be together. Surely, she remembers too. I close my eyes and I can still taste her sweet skin and her cum on my fingers. I can still recall the scent of her and the soft, sexy sounds she made when I took her first time. And then the desperate, needy little moans when she wanted more.

I imagine going into her room right now, peeling back the covers and spreading her legs wide for me before I run my palms up the smooth skin of her legs, and then getting my mouth on her pussy. I'd eat her until she came on my face, drinking up every drop of her release. My cock is painfully hard and I find my hand wrapped around the base, squeezing the shaft tightly, but it's not even nearly enough relief. No, the only relief for me would come from burying myself inside Addison Kinsella.

With a grunt of frustration, I roll onto my side and stare at the flames instead, trying to clear all the filthy thoughts of my best friend's sister from my head.

"DID YOU EAT MY TRAIL MIX?" She holds up the almost-empty packet. I distinctly remember being woken at 5 a.m. by one of the busted springs in that asshole couch and then feeling hungry. And her trail mix was right there on the counter. I was almost the entire way through the bag when I realized I should probably leave some for her.

"I'm sorry. I was hungry and...I thought all snacks were fair game."

She crosses her arms and that cute-as-fuck indignant look she gets settles over her face. God, she's gorgeous when she's mad. "The snacks *we* bought at the store are shared. Not *my* trail mix."

"I'm sorry. But I did leave you some."

She tips the contents of the packet out into her palm and a measly couple of unidentifiable brown things fall out. "Some? You call that some? Three nuts and a raisin. What am I, a squirrel?"

I raise a brow. "I thought after all the snacks we got yesterday you wouldn't miss your trail mix. I assumed you'd rather eat the double-chocolate-chip cookies you hid in the vegetable crisper."

I found her little stash last night after she stumbled to bed following our bourbon-tea confessions in front of the fire. And I'm relishing the look on her face now she knows she's rumbled. Her nostrils flare and her lips twitch. "Why don't you eat my ass, Chase!" she snaps.

Immediately, she realizes what she just said and the sheer horror that flashes over her face has me struggling to suppress my laughter. I expect her slip was a result of her not being able to decide whether to tell me to *eat my shorts* or *kiss my ass*. I have to take a minute to compose myself before I speak. "You want me to what now?"

She clamps her lips together, her eyes darting left and right like she's looking for the nearest exit. The wise move would be to come clean and admit that it was a slip of the tongue, but she's Addie, so she doubles down. Arms still folded over her chest, she looks me right in the eye when she says, "You heard me. Eat. My. Ass."

I pull out a stool, take a seat at the kitchen island and then tap the space on the counter right in front of me. "Come on over here then, baby. Sit your ass right here and I'll be happy to oblige."

Her eyes narrow, her lips twitch. "Don't be ridiculous, Chase. It's an idiom."

"No." I shake my head. "*Kiss* my ass is an idiom. Eat my ass is a request for a sexual favor, which as I've just stated, is a service I'm happy to provide." I tap the countertop again.

She snorts. "Sexual favor." And then she gives me

the eye roll, the one that makes my palm twitch with the desire to spank her ass.

"You don't think eating someone's ass is sexual? Or is it the favor part that you object to?"

Her glare could melt steel. She won't back down, but neither will I. I'm having far too much fun watching her squirm. We're both stubborn enough that we might just end up seeing this twisted game of ass-eating-chicken to its end. And the image of her on this counter with her juicy ass in my face is enough to have my mouth watering.

Her eyes dart between me and the countertop, and I'm certain she's actually considering jumping up there and taking off her pajamas and panties just to prove a point. But I would totally fulfill my end of this particular bargain. Not a doubt in my mind.

I can see her struggling, knowing if she doesn't back down, we will end up in a very compromising position. Eventually, she lets out a cute grunt of frustration. "Jackass!" she mutters and then storms out of the kitchen like a tiny tornado, leaving me to lament the distinct lack of ass in my mouth right now.

CHAPTER 14

CHASE

 # Never underestimate a man brave enough to wear Cuban heels

It's another day and another pair of heels. These are leopard print and they make her legs look even more incredible than usual. When I think she's not looking, I allow my eyes to rake over her entire body, but when they travel back up to her face, she's watching me with an amused look on hers.

"See something you like?" she asks.

I see *every-fucking-thing* that I like. "The shoes, Addie," is all I do say though.

"They're gorgeous, right?" She pops one leg up.

"They're fucking killing me," I mumble, quiet enough that she doesn't hear and when she asks what I said, I simply open the door and remind her we have dance rehearsals to get to.

SAMUEL BROWN, our dance instructor, is a former Broadway star and winner of the Vermont Starlight Award for Best Choreography by a Newcomer as he has advised us all at least five times in the past hour.

The steps for this particular number—which Brax and Eva would like their parents, the groomsmen and their partners, along with Addie and me, to perform after their first dance—aren't particularly difficult. However, both Brax and his dad appear to be getting it very wrong, at least according to the hellish screams coming from Samuel every five minutes. He's particularly focused on Brax, who in his loud opinion, "has the rhythm of a one-legged goat herder." I mean I didn't know that goat herders were particularly well-known for their lack of rhythm, but I don't keep up to date with all things dance related, so.

The dance is another idea of Eva's mom's. Apparently, it will make us all feel *involved* as well as encouraging everyone else to get their asses on the dance floor.

All I care about right now though, is that I'm staring into the eyes of the most beautiful woman in the world, and for the next few hours at least, I will have an entirely legitimate excuse to have my hands on her.

"Right, now we go again!" Samuel announces, clapping his hands. And a few seconds later the opening beats of "September" start playing—a song Eva's mom chose. I slide my hand to the small of Addie's back and take her left hand in my right one. I tug her a little closer, not close enough that she'll feel exactly how much I enjoy dancing with her, but close enough that her breath stutters a little. Then we grin at each other as Samuel loudly shouts out the steps.

"He's so intense," she whispers.

"I think he might have a fit if Brax or your dad mess up the steps again."

She snickers.

"Focus!" Samuel barks, clapping again. "Dancing is not supposed to be fun!"

Addie pulls a confused face and mouths, "Seriously?"

I make a shushing gesture with my lips before she gets us into more trouble, and the eye roll she gives me in return does something to me. Something that makes me want to bring her bratty side out to play. I glance around the room and confirm everyone is too focused on their steps to notice what we're doing. And I know I might be opening myself up to a swift kick in the balls here, but I do it anyway, I swat Addie's ass. A gentle tap, but enough for her eyes to blow wide and her mouth to drop open. She doesn't miss a single step though.

"Did you just?" she mouths.

"I warned you not to roll your eyes at me," I mouth back.

She presses her lips together, trying to look indignant, but her pupils are so dark it's hard to see the sparkling hazel of her eyes. Her lips twitch now, like she wants to smile, but daren't. The skin at the base of her neck turns a light shade of pink, the faint blush disappearing beneath the collar of her sweater—a place where I'd very much like to explore right now. I'd love nothing more than to see just how far that blush goes.

She tries to stomp on my standing foot with her heel, but I dodge her, and then maneuver her into a twirl, a move that was not sanctioned by Samuel and which therefore draws me a thorough scolding. I think this is the first time in my life I've been given a dressing down by a man in Cuban heels.

When Samuel is done berating me, Addie and I resume our scripted dance and she's practically vibrating from suppressing her laughter, and we resume our silent argument.

"That was your fault."

She tilts her chin, a smirk on her pretty face. "It was no less than you deserved."

I growl, yanking her body even closer to mine, and then I dip my head enough so that I can press my mouth close enough to her ear and speak without Samuel or anyone else hearing. "You, my naughty Firefly, deserve an actual spanking for that."

Her breath catches in her throat and I feel the shiver run through her body. She likes the sound of that, even if she's not going to admit it to me.

"And done!" Samuel announces. "Let us take a short break and then we will practice again."

Addie steps back, her eyes full of fire as they burn into mine. I'm probably going to hell for all of the things I'm currently thinking about doing to her right here in this dance studio, but that doesn't stop me from thinking them.

CHAPTER 15

ADDISON

Never ask questions you don't want to know the answers to

We had a lovely dinner after the dance rehearsals and I got to spend some time with Brax and Eva before they headed off to their cabin, barely able to keep their hands off each other as soon as they got out of the door. As happy as I am for them to have found their person, I can't help but feel a pang of envy too. Because why can't I find that? Chase was also with us, of course, and I will admit that it wasn't entirely terrible being in his company

After dinner, we walk back to the cabin, both of us fairly quiet. I assume he's tired, or full from dinner—or both. But I'm quiet because I'm not entirely sure what happened between us when we were dancing earlier. It definitely felt like he was flirting with me, and I'm sure I flirted back. Or are we just too familiar with each other that I can't decipher the difference between that and Chase just being Chase.

And what the hell does all of that even mean if it's true? Two days ago, I hated him. At least I spent eight years of my life convincing myself I hated him.

Clearly, I don't.

Clearly, I am losing my mind.

WHEN WE GET into the cabin, Chase lights the fire in the living room, and I make some tea. Ginger for me. Rooibos for him.

I add a small shot of bourbon to each and then we sit in front of the fire, each of us staring into the flames and a ton of unspoken tension between us. When I can't bear the silence any longer, I take a sip of tea and find the courage to speak. "So, the spanking?" I blurt out.

He smirks at me, an eyebrow raised in amusement. "You liked the sound of that, did you, Firefly?"

Yes, I did, but I will never admit that aloud to you. "No, I mean the actual spanking. You smacked my ass while we were dancing."

He shrugs. "You rolled your eyes. Did I or did I not warn you there would be consequences if you kept doing that?"

"Yes, but I didn't think you actually meant it."

He turns a little in his seat, like he's giving me his full attention. "I don't say things I don't mean, Addie."

I know those words weren't intended to hurt me, but my heart splinters open anyway. "Well, we both know that's not true, don't we?"

He takes a swig of his tea and then sucks on his top lip, staring into the flames once more. "I truly am sorry, Addie. I was a huge fucking asshole. I betrayed you and even worse, I made you feel worthless, and I will never forgive myself for that. But that was a long time ago, and I promise you I've changed."

The image of him with her, touching another girl while his cum was still inside me, is burned into my conscious for all eternity. I've tried so hard and so many times to erase it, but it's always there, like the image of an x-ray seared into my brain.

"Why did you do it, Chase?" All these years and I realize I've never actually asked him why.

He blows out a breath and then he just stares at me

for what feels like an eternity. "For the longest time I convinced myself that it was because I wasn't thinking straight. It was my second Christmas without my mom and I was..." He scrubs a hand over his face. "I was an asshole, Addie. I was drinking a lot. Screwing any girl who smiled at me. But none of it even touched taking the edge off that pain. And then there was you..." His Adam's apple bobs as he swallows hard. "And I felt something for the first time since my mom died, and it scared the hell out of me. When Hayley came to my place, I told her we were done for good. And then she asked if we could have one more...she took off her clothes and I..."

I watch the range of emotions flickering over his face like the reflection of the flames in the hearth.

"There's no excuse. I like to think I'd have come to my senses and told her to leave before things got too far, but I honestly don't fucking know if that's true. She asked me to fuck her and I ... I guess a fucked-up part of me wanted to feel that same connection to her that I had to you, even though I knew it was impossible."

He stops looking into the flames and turns to me, his eyes so dark they no longer look blue at all. "I have no excuse for acting like such an insensitive fuck-knuckle."

I sit with the information, and if I'm honest, it's

what I always expected he would say if I ever got the chance to ask. I've known Chase for so long, and I'm aware of how conflicted he must have felt after our night together. I was Brax's little sister, and our history together was a complicated one. "I almost forgave you, you know," I croak out the words as the memories come rushing back to the surface.

He blinks.

"I knew that you were hurting over your mom, and I knew that Hayley was desperate to win you back after she'd come all the way to Juniper Ridge to see you, so I went back to your place later that afternoon."

His eyes grow wider and he swallows hard.

"I wanted to talk to you and see what was going on in your head. I was stupid enough to want to give you a chance to explain, even after what you did."

"Addie!" His voice is as raw as the memories assaulting me.

"You were with Freddie. I heard you talking..." I leave that hanging in the air.

His face crumples. "Addie, no."

I nod. "I heard it all, Chase."

CHAPTER 16
CHASE
EIGHT YEARS AGO

I'm sure I should be feeling guilty right now. I mean I just had sex with my best friend's little sister, and if that didn't make me enough of a jackass, it was also her first fucking time. Not that I had any idea Addie was a virgin, and not because I have any particular reason to think she's not—other than she's smart and beautiful and there must be hundreds of guys at her college who've asked her out. And it's easy not to think about her dating other guys when she's in Boston and I'm in LA, but whenever I'm back home and I see her talking to other guys, I get this crazy jealous feeling that I try to pass off as being her concerned older brother's best friend, but I know it hasn't been that for at least a year now. And lately, whenever I spend any time in her company, I'm increasingly finding myself

136

thinking about what it would be like to kiss her, touch her. Fuck her.

And now I know.

And now my head is racing with questions and what ifs, and how the fuck I'm going to tell Brax I'm dating his sister. Because we will be dating. What happened last night wasn't a casual hookup. I knew that going into it, and now, now that I've felt her nails scraping down my back, kissed her perfect mouth, now I know I'm doomed.

But what if she doesn't want more? She said she didn't want things to be awkward, but that doesn't necessarily mean she wants to take this thing between us further. Maybe she just wanted her first time to be with someone she trusted. Fuck, what if I read it all wrong!

And then there's Hayley. We're over and we have been for months, but she gave up Christmas with her family to follow me here to Juniper Ridge—a place she's previously referred to as the "ass end of nowhere"—to try and make us work. And even though I contemplated giving us another shot, I already knew it was pointless. Being with Hayley is easy—but it's also fucking boring. Being with Addie—it feels like racing headfirst into a volcano on a motorcycle and not knowing if you'll brake on time. It's exhilarating like that, but it's also familiar and comfortable in a way things never were with anyone else. Addie is the first person to have made me feel anything remotely close to real since my mom died. I've always loved her and last night made me realize that those feelings are definitely not just platonic.

And what the fuck does that mean? I'm twenty-two years old and I just left college to start my dream job as an architect. Addie's only nineteen and in her sophomore year. We're both way too young to be thinking about forever...

"Chase," Hayley's voice cuts through the swirling vortex of thoughts currently racing around my head.

Immediately, I feel guilty. She obviously stayed at my house last night and knows I wasn't there.

"Hey."

"Where have you been?' she asks softly.

"I stayed with a friend."

"A girl?"

I could lie and spare her feelings, but it's better she knows there's no hope for us, and I tell her yes.

She shivers in the cold. "Can we go inside and talk?"

Talking to her is the least I can do, so I nod my agreement and we both head into my house. I leave her at the foot of the stairs, telling her I'm just going to go up to my room and change, and then I'll be right back.

The floorboards creak as I'm pulling off my T-shirt

and when I spin around, Hayley is in my room. "I thought you were—" I stop mid-sentence when she peels off her sweaterdress and drops it onto the floor, revealing she's not wearing a bra. "Hayley, what the hell are you doing?"

"I'm just asking for one more time, Chase. Let me remind you how good we were together and then if you still don't want me, we can go our separate ways."

What? No! This feels like a trick. Or a test. "I just told you I spent the night with someone else."

"I don't care, Chase. I need this from you, please? Just let me remind you how good it can be." She peels off her panties and I take a few steps back until I bump up against the bed.

I sit down and she stalks toward me and all I can think about is Addie. How much I've become infatuated with her. Our incredible night together. What the hell that means not just for me and her, but for me and Brax too.

"Please, Chase." Hayley's voice reminds me she's in the room. "It's the least you can do seeing as how I gave up Christmas with my family for you."

I didn't ask her to do that; in fact, I specifically asked her and Freddie not to follow me to Juniper Ridge. Her guilt trip won't work with me, but I can't deny that being with her would be easier. No feelings involved. No commitment. More importantly, there's no chance of her ever breaking my heart the way that Addie could. It's taken me a year to start to feel anywhere close to normal again after losing my mom, if feeling numb could be described as normal anyway. But Addison Kinsella makes me feel so much, and that means she could tear me to shreds. I'm not sure I'm ready for that kind of love...or that kind of pain.

"Hayley. We can't do this," I say, but it's a feeble protest.

She straddles me and rubs her bare pussy over my jeans. "Yes, we can."

No, we can't. I love Addie. Addie with her musical laugh and her beautiful smile and her luscious curves. The woman who might not even want anything more from me and the same woman who could obliterate my heart. I'm not sure I'm strong enough to put it back together for a second time.

"Just fuck me, Chase," Hayley says, reminding me there's an easier, far less painful option right in front of me.

I do the unthinkable; I flip her onto her back and unzip my jeans. Then I don't stop her when she slides her hand into my boxers, or when she wraps her slender fingers around the base of my dick. If I close my eyes I can pretend she's Addie. And I'm thinking of my girl even as I grind into my ex's hand. Addie's tight heat. Addie's soft skin. Addie's needy moans. "So good," I moan, recalling how incredible she felt last night.

"See, I told you how good we are together," Hayley says, running her free hand through my hair.

"Chase!" Now I even hear Addie's voice.

Fucking fuck! I turn my head and see my girl standing there, tears rolling down her face. My heart splinters into a thousand shards.

I jump off Hayley like she's on fire, but it's too late and Addie is already running down my stairs. "Addie, please! I can explain," I plead.

She spins on her heels, her eyes filled with fury like I've never seen. She tosses my wallet at me and I remember I left it at her place last night.

"I know you keep your mom's picture in there, and how much that means to you, so I brought it straight to you." She scrubs at the tears on her face. "Not that you deserve it."

"Addie I was..." I stop speaking. There is *no* excuse. No reasonable explanation for what I just did. Bile surges up from my stomach, burning the back of my throat.

"You were what? Screwing some other girl while your dick was still wet!" she snarls, pure venom in her tone. "You're disgusting. How could you?"

I step closer, wanting to wrap her in my arms and tell her how much I wish I could undo what I just did, but she backs away from me, edging toward the door. "Don't you dare come near me."

My heart feels like it's disintegrating in my chest. A deep physical ache that I already know can never be fixed. "I'm sorry, I didn't mean to..." I stop speaking because there's nothing at all I can say. No absolution for breaking the heart of the only girl I've ever loved.

"What happened to you, Chase? You used to be so smart and kind and fun, and now...now you don't seem to care about anyone but yourself. Your mom would be ashamed of you."

She turns around and yanks open the front door. As much as what she just said hurt, she's also fucking right. "Addie, please!" I try one more plea, running outside after her. The rain is coming down hard and has turned the snow on the ground into an icy mush. I slip in my bare feet, my knee almost buckling before I quickly right myself.

She gives me one last glare over her shoulder, and this one is all ice. Colder than the snow biting into my toes. "Go back to LA, Chase. It's where you belong. And if you ever come back to Juniper Ridge, I'll drive a fucking stiletto right through your heart."

She runs away from me and I take a few steps after

her, my feet struggling to find purchase in the slush on the ground, which means she's currently way faster than I am. So, I stand in the street and can do nothing but watch her walk away from me. At least the freezing rain running down my face disguises my tears, but it's no consolation when I know in my heart that I just made the biggest mistake of my entire life.

I SIT on the sofa with my head in my hands, not knowing how my day got so fucked up so quickly. Well, except for the fact that I almost screwed Hayley when my dick was still covered in Addie's cum. I can't even recall the conversation with Hayley that immediately followed, except that she left and we're done. So, there's that.

Freddie, who obviously did not leave with Hayley, but who is even less welcome here, flops onto the sofa beside me and starts rolling himself a joint. "Saw Hayley leaving town. She looked pretty upset."

"Yeah." I don't feel like discussing anything with him. The only person in the entire world I want to talk to hates my guts, and I can't blame her.

"You're a fucking asshole letting Hayley Steinbeck go, you know that. She is hot as fucking hell."

She's colder than ice compared to Addie's warmth and fire. "Yeah, well you go date her then."

He snorts, oblivious to my annoyance or my heartbreak. "So, where the fuck were you last night, man?"

"Out."

"Yeah. With who?"

I should tell him to get the fuck out of my house but I'm not sure I have the energy to argue with him. "Nobody you need to concern yourself about."

He's quiet for a few minutes and then he bursts out laughing. "You banged that chick, right? Your best buddy's sister?"

This seems to amuse him to the point of hysteria and he doubles over.

Rage burns hot and fierce in my chest. "What the fuck is so funny, Freddie?"

"Just imagining your buddy's face when I tell him you defiled his baby sister."

What the fuck? I should knock his goddamn teeth out. "I didn't *defile* her, and why the fuck would you tell him that?"

He shrugs. "Why wouldn't I? Unless she meant nothing to you and then we can go back to LA and get out of this shithole."

I swallow down the anger and hurt. The truth is, I do want to get out of Juniper Ridge, but only because

144

the sole reason I'm back here is to spend Christmas with the Kinsellas. And that's clearly a place I'll no longer be welcome. I can't bear to have to look my best friend in the eye and tell him how I betrayed his sister and broke her fucking heart. So, I tell Freddie what he wants to hear. "Of course it meant nothing." The words cut me open, but I force them out anyway.

"You sure about that?" he goads me.

I'm sure I want to end this fucking conversation. "Yes, I'm fucking sure, Freddie. She was desperate for a hookup and I threw her a bone. We can catch the next flight back to LA. Now fucking drop it. Okay!"

He gives me a shit-eating grin and it creeps me the fuck out. I need to drop him too.

I lean back against the couch and close my eyes. I cannot believe I just told him that and now it adds to the giant knot of guilt and regret and shame sitting right in the pit of my stomach. The look on Addie's face when she saw me with Hayley will haunt me for the rest of my days. I had the best girl in the entire world and I let her slip through my fingers. What the fuck is wrong with me?

Maybe Addie was right. My mom would be ashamed of me. What exactly am I doing with my life?

CHAPTER 17

CHASE

 # Don't pick open old wounds and expect them not to bleed

I f I ever had a heart, then it belonged to Addison Kinsella, and she just eviscerated it. No, actually she didn't. I eviscerated it myself eight years ago.

I recall that day so vividly. The guilt of what I did with Hayley. The pain on Addie's face when she caught us in my bed. Standing in the freezing rain, watching her literally run from me. I'd never felt so thoroughly shit about myself before or since—until now anyway. Because after Hayley left, I made it one hundred times fucking worse, and my only solace was that Addie hadn't heard those awful things I said. I can recall Freddie's smug face and how I wanted to punch him. I should have. Maybe then I wouldn't have told him the worst lie I've ever told anyone. The words that I know must have broken Addie's heart.

Addie takes a deep breath, tears shining in her hazel eyes. "I heard you tell your buddy Freddie that what we did meant nothing to you. How I was *desperate* for someone to hook up with and so you *threw me a bone*."

Her words—or rather mine, from her mouth, lance through my heart, sharper than a shard of glass. I'd had no fucking idea she'd heard that...and if I had, I would have begged for her forgiveness a long time ago.

I'm too stunned, too full of shame, too overwhelmed to speak.

She wraps the blanket around herself and stares into the fire. Protecting herself from me and from that memory that still obviously causes her so much pain. Of course it fucking does. It pains me more than I can bear, so I can't begin to imagine how much hearing me tell someone our first time together meant nothing must have hurt. It felt so very fucking wrong to say those words about her, and had I known she heard them... What would I have done? The truth is, I have no fucking idea. I was too messed up to deal with anything, and I was nowhere near a good enough man for her. It's still no excuse though.

"I'm sorry, Addie." The words aren't even close to enough, but they're all I have.

She sniffs. "Like you said, it was a long time ago."

"No. Don't make this easy on me. What I said is unforgivable..." I let those words hang in the air between us.

I could tell her that I didn't mean a word of it but I'm not sure it matters to her now. The fact is, she believed I meant those horrible things I said for the past eight years. When she was already vulnerable and hurting, I caused her more pain than I can even bear to imagine.

Guilt and regret ball into a thick knot in my throat and I can't swallow past them. I don't know how to move past this, although I do know I need to figure out a way to at least try.

CHAPTER 18

ADDISON

 # Never leave the house without your lucky shoes

"There we go, all in." Chase slams Angelina's trunk after packing all of the wedding flowers back inside, ready for us to drive to the main lodge. Things were a little awkward at breakfast this morning after our conversation last night, but actually I feel lighter for telling him what I heard him say. Like I can finally let it go.

Today, I'll be mostly setting out the arrangements on the tables, and that's good with me as I could do with a little break from the constant talking to people. It's not that I'm unsociable, but sometimes I just struggle making small talk. So, a few hours to myself, making beautiful flower arrangements is exactly what I need. In fact, it sounds like heaven.

Chase stands with his arms folded across his chest and a look of pride on his face over his ability to pack everything so tidily. I have to admit I did enjoy watching him load the car, if purely from an aesthetic perspective. Who doesn't enjoy looking at bulging biceps and rippling forearms? "You ready to go?" he asks, snapping me from my thoughts about his physique.

"Sure, just let me grab my shoes."

I slip on my heels and walk out of the cabin and he gives me a once over that he doesn't even attempt to hide this morning. I'm wearing my black heels today and I pop my leg up for him. "Do you approve?"

He nods. "Although, I think I prefer the red ones."

"Oh, you do? Well, I'm saving them for tonight. They go perfectly with my dress."

He mumbles something that I don't quite catch, but when I ask him what he said, he ushers me into the car and tells me we need to leave.

Brax and Eva were waiting outside the lodge for us when we arrived and we all unloaded the car together, and now we're standing in the huge main banquet hall, where the wedding's going to be held, along with the rehearsal dinner tonight. Currently, it looks bare, filled with tables and chairs but no personal touches. Like a blank canvas—full of potential and opportunity.

"Are you sure you don't need any help with all of this, Addie?" Eva asks me. "It looks like it's going to be a huge job. It's going to take you all day."

Yes, I know it is, and that's exactly how I want it.

"You're going to miss the games day Eva's mom has set up for us," Brax adds.

Yes, I also know this! Chase catches my eye and grins and I have to look away to stop myself from grinning right back. "I don't need any help and yes, I'm aware it's going to take a while, but this is what I do. And I love doing it. So, can you all go and leave me to create something magical?"

"What about food?" Eva asks. "You'll join us for lunch, right?"

I shake my head. "Just toss me some snacks and water at some point. I'll be fine."

"You're sure?" Brax asks.

"Yes!" I don't hide my exasperation any longer. "Now I don't want either of you to see this until the rehearsal dinner tonight, so go. Scoot. Leave."

"The hotel staff said they've left all the things you asked for." Eva nods to a corner filled with folded linens and, I hope, bazillions of string lights.

"Great."

Brax gives me a hug. "Good luck, sis. And thanks for this." He and Eva leave, but Chase hangs back for a moment.

"Don't you dare ask if you can help me. I am not being your pass to get out of *games day*," I warn him.

He smiles, that adorable one that makes my knees wobbly. "I would never. But if you need anything at all, let me know. Okay?"

"I will. Thanks."

"I can't wait to see you work your magic, Firefly."

AFTER CHASE LEFT, I immediately set to work, pleased that the hotel had indeed provided me with all of the extras I needed, including all the string lights my little heart desires. Ten minutes after I started work, a waiter came in bearing a tray of water, juice, pastries, cookies and fruit, which was very thoughtful, and I suspect Chase's doing. The eucalyptus sprigs have been particularly mischievous today and the table centerpieces took longer than I'd anticipated, but I've made great progress, and the entire room looks fit for a wedding now.

I stand on the stage where the band will be playing tomorrow night and admire my handiwork. The cream silk organza tablecloths and chair covers make the room look elegantly classy without detracting from the rustic theme of the lodge. I don't like to blow my own trumpet, but the flowers look truly beautiful. The whole room is blooming with white silk cala lilies and ranunculus, with a sprinkling of ruby-red roses for just a pop of color.

"Am I allowed to come in?" Chase calls.

"Are you alone?"

"Yes."

"Then you may enter."

He steps into the room, already dressed in his suit for dinner and I realize I'm probably not going to have time to shower and change now. I check my watch and realize dinner is only thirty minutes away. Dammit!

"Wow! Addie, this place looks incredible." Chase's awestruck voice reminds me why I did this. So what if I attend the rehearsal dinner in a different outfit than I intended to? I'm still wearing a dress, even if it is a sweaterdress. I'm already wearing heels. I can freshen up in my parents' room and borrow a little of my mom's mascara. "Seriously, this is fucking beautiful."

"You haven't seen the best part yet," I tell him. Then I flick the switch on the stage and the entire room lights up with thousands of twinkling lights.

"What the..." He stands in the center of the room

and spins around. "How did you even do all of this on your own?"

I shrug. "I told you, it's what I do."

I step down from the stage and join him. The room truly does look beautiful and I feel a rush of pride. "Later all of the jars in the middle of the tables will be lit too."

He swallows. "Brax and Eva are going to love it." Then his bright blue eyes find mine. "This is something else. You are fucking incredible, you know that?"

I blush. "Thank you. How was *games day*?"

He pinches the spot between his brows together. "Jesus Christ. It was brutal. You know how competitive your dad and his brothers get. And then your aunt Irene accused Eva's cousin of cheating at charades. It was quite possibly some of the worst few hours of my entire life."

I giggle. "Well, at least it's over now. And you look very handsome in your suit, by the way."

He smiles. "Thanks."

"I hope you don't mind sitting next to me when I'm a little dusty," I laugh, brushing some from my dress.

"I hope you don't mind that I went back to the cabin and got your dress and your red heels. I also picked up what I think was your makeup bag but I didn't look inside to check. They're all in your mom's room. She has some warm ginger tea and a hot shower waiting for you. And your aunt Irene says it will take her *like three and a half minutes* to curl your hair. And the caterers have confirmed we can push the dinner back by fifteen minutes if we need to."

My heart swells in my chest. "You arranged all that for me?"

He steps closer and does that thing where he rests just one finger under my chin and tips my head up, yet I feel his touch over my entire body. "It was the least I could do while you were doing this for everyone else."

"Thank you, Chase."

"Before you go." His throat works as he swallows. "I need you to know that I didn't mean any of it, Addie."

And now I'm confused, but he goes on speaking before I have a chance to ask what he's talking about. "The things I said to Freddie are unforgivable, but they were also outright fucking lies. That night I spent with you was...it was the best fucking night of my life, Addie. And no matter how scared I was feeling, or how much I thought I'd already fucked it up between us, I had no excuse for saying any of it. That you've believed what we did meant nothing to me all these years hurts me more than I can fucking bear, but I know that's not even a fraction of the pain you must have felt. I don't deserve your forgiveness, and I'm not asking for it, but I would hate to never get the chance to tell you how truly fucking sorry I am."

My heart is racing so fast my head spins. I don't even know what to say to that, but I do know I believe him. "I wish you'd told me that a long time ago."

"I do too, Firefly."

"Lightning bugs in a jar," I whisper.

He smiles. "Remember when I used to catch them for you?"

Yes, I do. He would catch them and I'd sit and stare at them for half an hour until he insisted that we let them go. It's why he calls me Firefly. Tears burn behind my eyes. No matter what he did, Chase Hunter will always be a part of me, and despite the heartbreak, my life is richer for having had him in it. "That's what the table decorations are supposed to be. Lightning bugs in jars."

"They're going to be perfect, Addie. Just like you." We stare at each other for the longest time, the moment stretching out between us and I'm not sure I ever want it to end.

Until I remember the dinner. "I have to get ready!"

"You have to get out of here," he says at the same time.

It breaks the tension at least. "Can you turn on all

the table lights before Brax and Eva come in? The lights are battery powered and the switch is inside the jar."

He nods. "Anything for you."

Does he truly mean that? I don't have time to ask. I have a rehearsal dinner to get ready for. I run out of the room and leave him to make the lightning bugs in jars happen for me.

CHAPTER 19

ADDISON

 # One kiss is all it takes...to ruin your life

Eva dabs at the corners of her mouth with her napkin, having finished the last drop of her champagne from the rehearsal dinner. "So, how's it going sharing a cabin with Chase?"

I'm immediately suspicious. "Why? What has he told you?"

She laughs and shakes her head. "Nothing at all. But why are you so defensive, Addie?" Her eyes are sparkling with mischief.

"I'm not defensive," I insist—defensively.

"Okay." Then she sighs. "It's just..."

"Just what?" I take a sip of my champagne, careful not to drink more than one glass because I have to drive Angelina back to the cabin.

"I always thought you and he would be perfect for each other, you know? I used to fantasize about how cool it would be if all four of us were in couples." Then she pulls a horrified face. "Obviously, I mean me and Brax and you and Chase."

"Yeah, I got that. But why would you think that? I mean, Chase is Chase. He's always been...well, Chase Hunter." Aka an unattainable godlike creature.

"I don't know. I know you used to have a crush on him back in high school, and then sometimes I used to see the way he looked at you and I wondered. And then he..."

Then he broke my heart into a million tiny fragments and never came back to Juniper Ridge again. It was Eva who found me that afternoon, crying in my bedroom. Well, not exactly crying, more like hyperventilating and having a full mental breakdown. I lied and told her it was about some guy from college rather than face the humiliation of Chase being the one who'd betrayed me so badly. I was ashamed to have been so wrong about someone I'd always looked up to and trusted.

"I always thought he'd move back some day, you

know? When we were kids, he always talked about growing old in Juniper Ridge. We all did."

"People change, I guess."

She nods and then wraps an arm around me. "Not you. You've always been so wonderfully you. I love you, Addie."

Well, now I'm crying. I brush away the tears before anyone sees. "Love you too, Eva. I'm really really happy you're marrying Brax."

She's crying now too. "Yeah, me too."

Speaking of whom, he walks up behind us, sliding an arm around each of our shoulders. "You two okay here?"

Eva sniffs. "Yes. Just telling your sister how much I love her."

That makes my brother smile, and he kisses her head and then mine. "The hall is truly something else, Addie. Thanks."

Eva nods her agreement. "It's stunning, Addie."

"Thank you. It's the least I could do for both of you."

"And this rehearsal dinner went so fucking well, I'm kind of scared that all the fuckups will happen tomorrow now." Brax lets out an anxious laugh.

"They absolutely will not," I assure him. "Dinner went well because why would it not? Tomorrow is going to be just as perfect."

Brax loosens his tie. "So long as Samuel doesn't berate me in the middle of our first dance for missing my steps."

Eva snickers.

"Don't worry, Chase and I will keep an eye on him for you."

"Did I hear my name being taken in vain?" He sits beside me.

"We were talking about how great today was and how tomorrow is going to be even better," I tell him.

He nods, smiling at his two best friends, who are now looking at each other in that way that makes me want to hurl. Mere seconds later, they excuse themselves and head back to their cabin, having announced they will absolutely not be following the tradition of spending the night before their wedding apart. Can't say I blame them to be honest.

"You want to head back too, Firefly?"

"Yes. I need a bourbon."

Chase stands and then he takes my hand, helping me up from my seat. I don't think I'll ever not react to the touch of his skin on mine, like electricity sizzling through my veins. When he lets go, I feel the loss of his warmth so acutely that it's almost like a physical hurt. I wonder if I'm just letting Eva's fantasy make me feel melancholy, but the truth is, it's a fantasy I've had many times myself.

WE DROVE BACK to the cabin in silence and as soon as we arrived, Chase jumped out of the car and came to open my door, once again taking my hand and helping me up. And I get that same feeling I always do, but this time he doesn't let go, his fingers clasped tightly around mine.

He's still holding on when we get inside and he closes the door.

"Thank you for your help today, by the way. And dinner was fun."

"I would do anything for you, Addie. And yes, dinner was fun. Mostly because you were there. Actually, I just really enjoy spending any time with you." His voice is thick with emotion.

"Me too," I whisper.

We move closer, and once again I find myself standing like this with him—staring into his blue eyes, our bodies so close together I can feel the heat from him through our clothes. His gaze rakes over me, a subtle caress on my skin that sends a shiver of excitement skittering up my spine.

He dips his head and his lips brush so softly over

mine that I hardly feel them, yet somehow, I experience that barely-there kiss more deeply than I've felt anything in a very long time.

"Fuck, Addie," he groans.

It would be so easy to give into this and let him make me feel the kind of pleasure I know only he is capable of. But he can cause me pain like nobody else can too, and even if I trust he wouldn't hurt me on purpose this time, I have no idea how I'd feel tomorrow morning in the cold light of day. What if I make another huge mistake?

It takes a gargantuan feat of willpower, but I pull away from him. "We can't do this, Chase. And especially not the day before Brax and Eva's wedding. What if we mess something up for them? I would never forgive myself."

He sighs, but it's one born of realization. "I know, Firefly. Me too."

I stare at the tiny couch he's been sleeping on this week and feel a pang of guilt. "You still don't have to sleep on that couch tonight though."

"Addie!" He says my name like it pains him.

"Look, you need to be at your best tomorrow, right? That couch is way too small for you. We can share a bed without mounting each other, can't we? We're not animals."

He tilts his head to the side, like he's considering that and I nudge him in the arm. "We can even put a wall of pillows between us if you think that would help?"

He laughs. "You're sure you can sleep next to me and resist *mounting* me?"

No, I am absolutely not sure. "I think I can handle it," I tell him instead.

CHAPTER 20

CHASE

 # Never assume her red flannel pajamas will be any kind of prevention against unwanted erections

I'm both relieved and disappointed to see that she's wearing pajamas for bed. And they are quite the pajamas—red tartan flannel monstrosities festooned with dogs in Santa hats—but on her, they're fucking adorable. I have no idea how the fuck I'd keep my hands off her if I could see any of her skin given how much of an effort it is when she's covered from head to toe in flannel. She stares at me through her dark lashes and I ball my hands into fists to stop myself from touching her. But I think about it. I think about rolling on top of her and letting my hands wander over every goddamn inch of her flawless skin. And then I'd do the same with my mouth, until she was writhing beneath me and begging me to fuck her. I still recall how sweet she tasted. How her snug pussy squeezed tight around me when I took her first time. How she moaned out my name and raked her nails down my back when she came for me. How she woke me for more in the middle of the night and then fell asleep in my arms afterward.

My stiff cock throbs.

"What are you thinking about?" she whispers.

"Whether Samuel is going to have a heart attack tomorrow if Brax gets his steps wrong again." I lie with ease.

She giggles and it's so damn adorable that I want to kiss her. Sharing a bed was a mistake. I'm going to spend the entire night with a painful hard-on.

"Do you regret me being your first, Addie?" I ask, unsure where that question came from, and why the hell I want to put myself through such torture. But it seems like this has been a day of opening up old wounds, maybe healing some too if we're lucky. Maybe we can become friends again, even though what I'd like is so much more.

Her brows pinch together in a cute-as-fuck frown,

like the kind she used to have when I'd help her with calculus. Eventually she answers me, "Yes and no."

Okay, that could have been worse. Could have been better too. "Care to enlighten me any further?"

"Well, that would require me being vulnerable with you, Chase. Can I do that?"

I nod. "You can trust me, Firefly. You can tell me anything, even if it hurts."

She chews on her lip for a second. "For a long time, I would tell myself that what we did was a huge mistake. I think it made it easier to deal with."

Well, that stings. We weren't a fucking mistake! I made a huge fucking mistake afterward, but that doesn't mean what happened was one. Sensibly, I keep my mouth shut and let her talk instead.

"But I don't think we were, were we?" Her voice cracks a little, like my heart.

As relieved as I am to hear her say that, it's gratitude I'm feeling more than anything else, grateful that she's allowing me to see this vulnerable part of her after I hurt her so badly.

"No, we weren't, Addie."

She smiles and I have to bite the inside of my cheek to stop myself from kissing her.

"So, no I don't regret that you were my first because

it was special and it was incredible. Even if it didn't mean all that much to you—"

"It meant something to me, Addie." I can't stop myself for interrupting her this time.

Now her eyes are wet with unshed tears. "But that's also why I regret it too. Because it meant so much, but what you did and said afterward...it kind of made it all mean nothing."

A tear runs down her cheek and she flicks it away before I have a chance to. "I'm not trying to make you feel bad about it anymore. I'm just explaining how I feel."

"I know, Firefly. And I deserve to feel bad."

She sniffs and shakes her head. "Not anymore, Chase. It was eight years ago. You were grieving. We were young." She rests a warm hand on my cheek. "I forgive you."

How do I tell her that I don't want her forgiveness, and not only because I don't deserve it—she was so innocent and trusting and she loved me so fucking much and I broke it—but also because this feels like she's letting me go.

She speaks before I have a chance to say any of the things I should tell her. "We'd better get some sleep. We have a big day tomorrow."

I can only nod, worried that if I speak, I'll tell her

how much I want her. Or how many times I have dreamed about that night and wished that it didn't still affect me after eight long years without her. There has never been anyone who could get under my skin like her. And we can pretend that it was just one night between us, but it was so much more. All the times we watched a movie together, or laughed at a stupid in-joke that only me and her understood. Every smile. Every lingering look. Every brush of skin. All the times she hugged me and I held on a little too long. Every second that we ever knew each other, leading to me falling in love with her.

Yeah, I fell in love with Addie Kinsella eight years ago, and I'm still in love with her now.

CHAPTER 21
ADDISON

 # If you're going to have a panic attack, make sure to do it in the vicinity of an annoyingly perfect demigod with sparkling blue eyes

I slept fitfully all night, a part of me worried I'd wake in the night with my body wrapped around Chase's and then I would have subsequently died of embarrassment, or begged him to fuck me. But neither of those outcomes would have been good. When I wake, the next morning though and find him lying flat on his back, one arm thrown over his face and the covers pulled down to his navel, I can't stop myself from staring for a few minutes. His abs should really come with some kind of government health warning.

"Are you awake?" he groans and I snap my eyes closed, pretending I wasn't gawking at him.

"I am now."

"What time do you have to be at Brax and Eva's for the hair and makeup stuff?"

"Eleven."

He pushes himself up onto one elbow, his dark hair falling into his eyes. "So, we have time for breakfast then?"

I nod and he smiles and then we just stare at each other for the longest time, and it feels way too intimate, but I can't help liking it. And I think about what it would be like if he leaned down and kissed me. How easily I would part my lips and welcome him inside. Or what if he had a total fuck-it moment, rolled on top of me and tore off my pj's. I'd probably still part my lips and welcome him inside—that thought makes me giggle and it seems to snap Chase from whatever thoughts he was having.

"You are far too dangerous to be lying in this bed with, Addie Kinsella," he says before jumping out of bed. "I'll go make a pot of coffee if you promise to make me some of your delicious pancakes."

I salute him. "You have yourself a deal, sir."

He groans, muttering curses to himself as he slips out of the bedroom.

EVERYTHING ABOUT BRAX and Eva's wedding day has been truly perfect. There's no better way to describe it. The champagne brunch with just me, Eva and our moms was perfect. Chase sneaking in to tell Eva how beautiful she was and how he was her best man too was perfect. Braxton and Eva's vows were perfect. Her hair and dress were perfect. We laughed. We cried. We drank champagne. We posed for a bazillion photographs, and I didn't even mind a little that Chase and I had to be in so many of them together. I didn't even mind when the photographer suggested he pick me up for one of them, and instead of the scooping up she suggested, he threw me over his shoulder.

He has also been perfect today. A sight to behold in his tuxedo, but more than that he's been charming and helpful and funny, and the Chase I always knew and loved.

The entire room is currently hanging on his every word as he delivers his best-man speech, which has thus far consisted of some hilarious stories involving Brax and Eva, and occasionally him, that have had all of the guests doubled over with laughter. "The truth is, I could tell you all a million more stories about Brax and Eva, and I know plenty more that are even funnier than the ones I've shared with you today. But I love them too much to dig up those skeletons. Not to mention incriminating myself."

Everyone laughs again.

"So, I'll just end with telling you all that they are two of my favorite people in the entire world, and I have never known two people more right for each other than they are." Chase raises his glass and we all do the same. "To Brax and Eva, I'm truly honored to have been a part of your journey here, and a part of this incredible day. I love you both so much and I could not be happier that you've finally officially made me the third wheel."

The entire crowd chants a toast and then erupts into cheers and wolf whistles. Chase simply smiles and takes his seat, always comfortable being the center of attention.

Unlike me. And I have to follow that.

My palms are sweaty. I take a long swig of my champagne and immediately regret it when the bubbles make my head spin. And now I'm in fifth grade again and Tommy Pierce is yelling at me to "hurry up and talk, fart-face" while I stand on the stage in front of the entire school.

I take a deep breath, but it doesn't work. Dammit. I have three minutes before I have to make my speech and I abhor public speaking. Now I have no idea why I ever agreed to this. Pushing back my chair, I make a quick apology and dash for the ladies' room.

I don't make it that far when he's behind me.

"Addie, are you okay?" Chase's deep voice stops me in my tracks.

I spin around and shake my head. "No. I can't do it, Chase. I've forgotten every single thing I was planning to say and I didn't make notes, because I practiced it like a bazillion times."

My heart is galloping in my chest and my breathing is getting heavier and faster. Sweat trickles down my back. Attractive!

"Addie." He takes my hands in his and places one on my chest, right over my heart, and one on his. "You're okay."

I shake my head. "I'm not."

"Yeah, you are." He steps closer. "Breathe with me. Okay?" He tips my chin up with his finger until I'm staring into his eyes and then places both of his hands over mine. "Breathe, Firefly."

I take a deep breath and then try to match the rise and fall of his chest. "What if I blow it and ruin their big day?"

"You won't."

It takes a moment, but my breathing evens out and my legs stop shaking. "I freaked out."

He hums. "I know. God, I should have kicked Tommy Pierce's ass."

That makes me laugh. "Well, he was a lot smaller than you. But you remember that?"

"Of course I do."

Of course he does. His little Firefly. There were so many times he was there for me, just like he is now. "You were there for almost all the important moments of my life, Chase. Good and bad."

He holds my gaze, eyes burning into mine like he's trying to reach inside my soul. "I'd like to be there for all the future ones too, Addie."

I'm not sure what he even means by that, but I know that I'd like that too. "Did you have to do such an incredible job back there?"

He smirks. "Can't help being so funny now, can I?"

I chew on my lip before I speak again. "If I mess up, will you help me out?"

He shakes his head. "You won't need my help. You're going to be incredible because you're going to speak from your heart and nobody loves those two as much as you do. All you need to remember is that everyone in that room cares about you. And plenty of them love the hell out of you too. You've got this, Addison Kinsella." He presses a tender kiss on my forehead that makes my knees tremble again, albeit for an entirely different reason than before. "You ready to go back in there and give the best speech by any person at any wedding ever?"

"Yes." How does he have the ability to soothe and inspire me all at the same time? He always has done, and it's like a superpower.

"That's my good girl," he murmurs.

Okay, well now my knees just actually buckled and the only reason I don't fall is because Chase is holding me up. "You okay?"

My cheeks are flaming with heat. No, not even a little okay. I almost passed out because you called me your good girl! I blow a strand of hair from face and lie my ass off. "I'm great. Let's go."

I shrug out of his grip, roll back my shoulders and remember I'm wearing my you-got-this red heels again today, and then I stride back into the reception. Aware that Chase is quite probably staring at my ass, I make sure to sway my hips for all they're worth and give him something to get hot under the collar about.

CHAPTER 22

CHASE

Always make friends with the band

A raucous cheer erupts when Brax and Eva take to the floor for their first dance and I cannot stop myself from smiling as I watch them together. Not only because they look so insanely happy and I'm thrilled for them, but because as soon as their first dance is done, then it will be time to do our rehearsed dance, and I will have a wholly legitimate excuse to have Addie in my arms while I stare into her eyes.

The band's soulful rendition of "To Make You Feel

My Love" ends and Brax and Eva kiss to a chorus of whistles and hollering. He dips her and she squeals.

"I remembered all my steps, and I got to dance with the most beautiful woman in the room," Brax declares and then he fist pumps the air.

I'd have to disagree with the latter part of his claim because I'm looking right at the most beautiful woman in the room—she's the most beautiful woman in any room. My heart rate almost doubles. Addie is on the opposite side of the dance floor and I watched her during Brax and Eva's first dance as much as I watched them. Her beautiful face lit up with delight the entire time.

"Can the wedding party please take to the floor for the next song?" one of the band members announces over the microphone.

There's another cheer.

I'm still staring at Addie. Now our eyes meet and I swallow down the thick knot of nerves. We've practiced this. It's just a dance, Chase.

She glides across the floor toward me, effortless even in the sky-high red stilettos. Fuck me, she is the most beautiful sight I ever saw. I will my dick not to get inappropriately hard when we dance in front of all these guests, but already he's ignoring me, twitching at the thought of having her so close.

I hold out my hand. "Shall we?"

She wraps her slender fingers around mine, warm and soft and right. And then I pull her into my arms and it feels like the most natural thing in the whole fucking world. One hand on the small of her back, I guide her around the dance floor, repeating the steps that Samuel drilled into us. We're one of a half a dozen couples but I'm only focused on her. The flickering lights reflected in her hazel eyes. The warmth of her skin beneath my palm. The scent of her perfume. Everything that is Addison Kinsella intoxicates me.

This is the last of our *duties* for this evening. Soon Brax and Eva will ride off to their cabin on the opposite side of the lake and probably not leave it for days, and this day will be over. And this thing will be over. A wave of sadness washes over me.

"Today went well, didn't it?" Her warm breath dusts over the skin of my neck, making the hair stand up on my nape.

"Yeah. You were great."

"So were you. Your speech was perfect."

You are perfect, Addison Kinsella. Something stops me from saying that—possibly the ever-present danger of a swift knee to my groin. "Thanks," I mumble instead.

And then we're silent, moving to the music until the

song ends. She bristles. Goes to pull away but I hold her tight. "One more dance, Addie. Please?"

She looks up at me, eyes shining. "Why?"

"Because I don't want to let you go yet."

She stares at me for the longest time, the moment stretching out for an eternity. And then she leans into me, resting her cheek against my shoulder. I dust my lips over her hair. And then she recognizes the song the band is playing right before the singer belts out the first line of "Santa Tell Me."

She looks into my eyes, and hers are shining with delight. "Did you ask them to play this song?"

"Yeah. I don't know if you remember, but you danced to it at Hugo's party."

"I remember. I also remember I was thinking about you when I did."

Oh, fuck me. I can see her now, a wicked smile on her face as she popped her hips and mouthed the words. "I'm so fucking sorry, Addie."

"I know." She smiles and then nestles her head against my chest once more, and I wrap her in my arms and enjoy the feel of her being here with me, right where she belongs. Her parents dance past us and Maggie gives me a knowing wink that makes me laugh.

The song ends all too soon and the singer

announces that the bride and groom are leaving, which is met with a chorus of wolf whistles and cheers.

"I guess we should go say bye," Addie says, and I reluctantly let my arms fall from around her waist.

"How about we pick up right here when we're done though?"

The smile she gives me makes my knees feel like they've been hit with a sledgehammer. "If you're a good boy."

WE ALL WAVE the newlyweds off in their golf cart as they prepare to spend the next four days holed up in their cabin. Brax has already warned everyone that we won't be hearing from them for at least forty-eight hours and I'm happier than I can ever put into words for him and Eva. I have to admit I'm happier about the fact that Addison just danced to a song with me that she wasn't signed up for. She chose to. And she didn't seem even the slightest bit uncomfortable in my arms, not even when she rubbed up against me and had to have felt how very hard for her I am.

We wait until almost everyone else has gone back inside, Addie staring off into the direction of the golf cart with a huge smile on her face. I slip my hand into hers. "How about that next dance?"

She giggles and the sound is so joyous and carefree, it's almost like we've turned back time to before I acted like the world's biggest asshole. "I think these heels were made for dancing."

We're almost back to the main lodge when someone calls out her name. And it makes every single hair on the nape of my neck stand on end, not to mention jealous, possessive anger burn in my veins.

What the fuck is he doing here and more importantly, did she invite him? I never did get to the bottom of why Eva found her crying into her wine over this guy. And she even admitted that she was cut up about not coming to the wedding with him. Even if he is a douchecanoe, maybe Jasper is the man she wants to be with.

The very idea makes me want to throw her over my shoulder like a caveman, carry her to our cabin and remind her exactly who she's always belonged to.

CHAPTER 23
ADDISON

 # Always take the win and walk away—aka never poke the angry bear

T twist around, sure I must have imagined hearing him shouting my name, but no, there he is... dressed in a suit and tie.

"Jasper, what the hell are you doing here?"

He smiles sheepishly. I'm sure he thinks it makes him look adorable but actually it makes him look like a naughty schoolboy. "I made a mistake, Sugarmuffin. And I knew how much it meant for me to be here with you." He glances around. "At your brother's wedding."

"The wedding's over, fuck-face," Chase growls.

That's exactly what I was going to say, minus the fuck-face, but I throw Chase a warning glare anyway. "I've got this," I say through clenched teeth. "Can you give us a moment?"

He scowls at Jasper, his jaw working. "Nope, don't think I will."

"Chase, please?" I ask. "I can handle this. Please just go inside."

"I'm not leaving you out here alone with him, Addie," he insists.

"I can take care of myself. Now please go!" I level him with a look, and with a grunt of annoyance, he finally leaves us, muttering to himself as he stalks to the hotel lobby.

Jasper is still smiling, seemingly oblivious to Chase's disdain and the fact there is clearly some history between him and me. "Adders," he says sweetly.

A distant cousin bumps into me on her way back into the party, apologizing before she resumes her performance of the Cha Cha Slide.

I usher Jasper away from the doorway because I'd rather not have everyone I know witness me telling him to go home. There's every chance he might cause a scene. So emotional!

Jasper holds out his hands. "I'm here, Sugarmuffin. Just like I promised I would be."

184

"We broke up," I remind him. "Where is Lacey? She's the one who gets you, right?"

He winces like I've physically hurt him. "She wasn't quite the woman I thought she was. You know how it is."

I sigh. "What the hell are you doing here?"

"I want to give us another shot, Adders."

I shake my head. "No way. You cheated on me. In my own apartment!"

He takes a half step toward me. "It was a mistake, Adders. We all make mistakes."

"Nailing another woman on my sofa wasn't a mistake, Jasper, it was a calculated and spectacular fuck-you to what was left of our already crumbling relationship."

He scowls at me. "We were good together, Sugarmuffin. You know we were."

"Please never call me Adders or Sugarmuffin ever again. We weren't good, we were a train wreck. And you really need to leave."

"And not make use of the cabin we booked?" His lip curls and his eyes rake over my face before lingering on my boobs, which I now realize are very prominent in this dress. Chase hasn't ogled my boobs all day. Not once.

"Come on, Adders," Jasper croons. I'm sure he's

trying to be seductive or something, but he just looks creepy as hell. Does he really think...? Oh, God! I can think of nothing worse.

He grabs hold of my wrist and I try to wrench out of his grip, but he holds tighter, yanking me toward him until I stumble in my heels, falling into his chest. I plant a hand on his shoulder, trying and failing to push him away. "Take your hands off me. You're an asshole."

"And you're a dirty little slut. Come on, babe. We were good together and I know you still want me."

"You're a fucking dead man if you don't take your goddamn hands off her right now!" Chase growls and despite me asking him to go, I'm filled with relief that he's here.

Jasper releases me, but Chase already has him by the collar of his shirt. "And what the fuck did you just call her?"

Jasper's lip wobbles. "I didn't mean anything. She likes being called that...don't you, Adders?"

Chase doesn't wait for my reply; he simply punches Jasper in the face, knocking him on his ass.

Jasper looks at me, his lip bleeding and tears running down his cheeks. "Adders, please?"

Chase looks like he's about to dive on him and go another round, but I grab hold of his forearm. "Don't. Just leave him be."

"I love you, Adders," Jasper pleads.

I offer him a hand and help him up, while Chase growls his annoyance behind me. "Please go home, Jasper. I don't love you. I don't even like you. And stop calling me Adders!"

He looks furious and dejected, and if Chase wasn't here, I'm sure he'd plead his case some more. Maybe even grab hold of me again, but he's too much of a coward to do it with the angry six-foot-three-inch wall of Chase right behind me.

Instead, he drops his head, and saunters in the direction he came in. "Slut," he mutters.

Oh, Jasper! You absolute gold-standard, grade-A idiot. You were free and clear, and you just couldn't walk away without giving your dented ego a little boost. Chase moves so fast, he's almost a blur. In two strides, he has Jasper by the scruff of his neck, and the sight of my misogynistic ex-boyfriend being yanked back like a feral dog on a leash would almost be comical if I didn't abhor violence.

"You really are a stupid fuck, Jasper," he growls, and then his two hands are wrapped around Jasper's throat, and my ex-boyfriend is coughing and sputtering, his eyes bugging out of his head. Jasper is big guy, but Chase manhandles him like he's a ragdoll, forcibly dragging him over to me. He shakes Jasper hard. "Apologize to her."

Jasper chokes, and I'm sure he's unable to speak with the grip on his throat.

Chase shakes him again. "Now! Fuckface."

"S—sorry," Jasper sputters, face turning a deeper shade of purple with each passing second.

"Chase, you can let him go. Please? He's not worth it."

Chase snarls in the other man's face, causing Jasper to physically tremble. "Leave her the fuck alone, you dipshit. You ever call her that again, speak to her again, *look* at her again, and I will bury your body somewhere you will never be found. Do I make myself clear?"

Jasper jerks his head in a nodding motion. "Y— yeah."

Then Chase moves his mouth close to Jasper's ear. "Stay the fuck away from my girl, asshole," he says in a deep, low growl and I'm not sure if I was supposed to hear that, but the possessiveness in his tone has my entire body trembling, and now it has nothing to do with Jasper's behavior.

Chase shoves him roughly away and Jasper stumbles backward, rubbing at his throat. "Now, fuck off!" he growls.

This time, my ex-boyfriend gets the message and he slinks away in the direction he came from.

Chase is beside me in an instant. "Are you okay?" Gently, he takes my hand and inspects my wrist. "Did he hurt you?"

"No. I'm fine." It's a lie. Jasper showing up here out of the blue has freaked me out. And he scared me. He was always a little pushy when it came to sex, but there was a look in his eyes tonight that truly frightened me. "Thank you for coming to my rescue."

He slips an arm around my shoulder. "Always, Firefly. You want to go back inside and dance?"

I shake my head. "I don't feel like dancing anymore."

His eyes travel over my face and I'm reminded of the possessive words he spoke to Jasper just now, and how he called me his girl. Perhaps he was simply saying that to warn Jasper off, but it doesn't make the impact any less. "You want to go back to our cabin and finish that bottle of bourbon?" His voice is deep and seductive.

I nod. Nothing has ever sounded better.

CHAPTER 24

CHASE

 # Saran Wrap is not an effective method of contraception

I told Addie's parents we were leaving and then I draped my tuxedo jacket around her shoulders, ignoring the sass she gave me about *pretending to be a gentleman*. After all, there is nothing gentlemanly about the things I'd like to do to her when we get back to the cabin.

Nothing at all.

While we walk, she tells me about the time she was traveling in Europe and thought she'd got lost in a wood like this one, only to find she was behind a huge housing complex the entire time. She's giggling by the time we get through the door of the cabin, her cheeks flushed and her eyes sparkling. I close the door behind us and she leans against it, head tilted up and staring into my face.

I can't help it. All of the restraint I've been desperately holding onto crumbles. I eat up the distance between us, placing my forefinger under her chin so she can't look away when I tell her. "You are so fucking beautiful."

"Chase." She pants out my name on a breath. "We can't."

I dip my head lower, until her breath dances over my neck. Her breathing gets heavier. "Give me one good reason why not, Addie."

"I—I can't think of any," she whines, frustrated. "But we still shouldn't." Her hands fist in my shirt, pulling me closer, and now my hard length is pressed up against her abdomen. I know the moment she feels it because she gasps and her eyes dart downwards for a second.

"Can you feel what you do to me, Addie?"

"That's all because of me, huh?" she purrs.

"Who else would it be for, Firefly. I have spent the last four days with an almost-permanent hard-on." I dust my lips over her neck and she grinds her hips against me, making my cock ache with need. "Tell me to stop, Addie." It's a challenge and a plea. Because if we do this, it can't be undone. This time I won't fuck it up. I'm not letting her go a second time.

She tips her head back. "Don't stop, Chase."

That's all I need to hear. I smash my mouth against hers, fingers working quickly to pull up her silk bridesmaid dress enough to give me access to her soft skin. My hands coast over the supple skin of her thighs.

She whines. I move higher. Until I reach the delicate lace of her panties. I growl, filled with the burning need to take her right here. Roughly, I tug her panties aside and slide my fingers through her folds.

Fuck me, she's already soaked and I think I might come in my pants just from touching her. She fucking unravels me.

I sink a thick finger inside her tight pussy and am rewarded with a thick coating of her arousal.

"You're fucking soaked, Firefly."

"I know."

I work a finger in and out of her, all the while my cock aches to be inside her too. But I want to watch her fall apart for me first. I grind the heel of my palm against her clit and add a second finger to her tight heat. Her eyes roll back in her head. She claws at my suit jacket. Her muscles clench around me as her impending climax milks my fingers.

I press my mouth against her ear. "That's my good girl. You can let go. I've got you, baby."

She cries out as her orgasm tears through her, leaving her entire body trembling. Only when she's stopped do I slip my fingers out of her and suck them clean. She tastes just as good as I remember. Then I wrap her still shaking legs around my waist and carry her through to the bedroom. We fall into a heap on the bed, hands scrabbling to remove each other's clothes in our frantic need to get each other naked.

Soon our clothes are strewn around the floor; her bra is hanging from the bedside lamp and her panties on the dresser along with one of my socks, but I take a moment to stare at her—committing every inch of her sexy body to memory. Her full breasts and the curve of her hips to her perfect pussy. When we first had sex eight years ago, she was completely waxed, but now she has a thin, neat strip of short, dark curls down the center. Either way it's still the most beautiful pussy I've ever seen and she blushes when I tell her so.

She wraps her slender legs around my waist. "Do you have any condoms?"

"Why the hell would I have condoms, Addie?"

She chews on her lip and I rack my brains for an

alternative, because I'm sure I will have some kind of erection-related aneurysm if I don't fuck her soon. My Addie-addled brain immediately goes to the Saran Wrap in the kitchen before dismissing it just as quickly. "Are you on birth control?" I ask her instead.

She eyes me suspiciously. "Yes."

"Have you ever let anyone fuck you without a condom?"

She smiles sweetly. "Only you, asshole."

That pleases me more than she will ever know, but I have more pressing matters to deal with—specifically the tip of my dick against her sweet pussy. "And you are the only woman I've ever fucked bare, so—"

"No freaking way," she exclaims.

I frown, all the while my poor, aching cock is screaming at me to give him some relief. "Why is that so hard to believe when I believed you immediately?"

She wrinkles her nose. "Because you're a hound dog who's slept with way more people than I have."

I squeeze her ass and she yelps. "I am not a fucking hound dog." Her eyes narrow in suspicion and I take a breath and try again. "I know I let you down in the past, but I would never lie to you about something as important as this, Firefly, now for the love of all that is holy and sacred, can I please fuck you?"

"If you don't hurry up and fuck me, I'm not above

venturing into the dungeon and finding something else to do the job."

I drive inside her so hard, her head bangs against the headboard.

"Damn, that feels good," she moans.

It feels better than good. "You feel like fucking heaven."

CHAPTER 25

ADDISON

 # Apparently, fighting is the best foreplay there is

Wow!

Pleasure rockets through my core, lighting up my veins as Chase drives his giant dick inside me, over and over again. I never come from penetration alone, but maybe it's the incredibly intense orgasm he just gave me still lingering in my lady parts, or perhaps it's the four-day-long foreplay we've been indulging in, but whatever it is, he has me teetering on the knife edge of oblivion already.

"You're so fucking wet and tight, Addie," he groans, his hot mouth pressed right against my ear.

Or maybe it's the dirty talk. I love a vocal man, yet so often they don't know what to say, or they say the right thing at the wrong time. Not Chase Hunter, he has a master's degree in dirty talk, and I am so here for it.

I squeeze my pussy walls around his dick and it makes him grunt like an animal. "Jesus. Fucking. Fuck!"

Sinking my heels into the firm muscles of his ass, I pull him deeper inside me, even as I know there's no way he can get any further in there. I'm pretty sure he's hitting my cervix, but I want more. Crave more. I scratch my nails down his back and it seems to drive him even more feral. He slams into me. Harder and faster. And I cry out, bucking my hips to meet his thrusts. Like eight years of anger and tension and hurt are being poured into this one act.

"Fuck, Addie."

"Yes, Chase!" My core tightens and my inner muscles squeeze tight around him as an earth-shattering orgasm explodes out of my body. He drives into me one more time before his hips still, and he grinds into me, making me take every single drop of his release while he mutters a string of curses.

And while I take a moment to catch my breath, he sucks one of my nipples into his mouth and bites down gently, reigniting the sparks of pleasure still skittering inside me. And then his hand is between my thighs, his skilled fingers circling over my clit.

My body bucks against him.

"I'm too sensitive."

"I know you are, baby. Just give me one more."

"I c—can't," I protest, but already my eyes are rolling back in my head and my entire body is singing, desperate with the need to come.

He looks up at me, smirking. "You want me to stop?"

"N—no."

"Good girl." He sucks on my nipple and presses down on my clit; another climax tears through me, leaving me shaking and trembling.

No man on God's green earth has *any* right being as good at sex as Chase Hunter is. It should be forbidden by the laws of nature for one single person to make another person come so many times in such a short space of time.

It should be, but it's not.

"Chase!" I pant out his name as he trails that wickedly sinful mouth down my body.

"I haven't tasted you yet, Addie, well except for off my fingers, but I know your pussy is going to be so much sweeter than that."

I sink my head back into the pillow, too wrung out

to protest, and also enjoying what his mouth is doing far too much. So, I give over to the pleasure and let him take full control.

And when his tongue licks a firm path along my wet center, I moan his name, entering a whole new world of ecstasy. Then he does something with it that has my toes curling and my hands fisting in the sheets. "You really do have a filthy mouth," I pant.

"How about you make it even filthier for me, baby, and come on my face?"

It can be no more than a few minutes later when I happily oblige him. And I'm still in my post-orgasm bliss when he's kissing my neck and sliding his rock-hard cock inside me again.

Chase is a machine. And I'm going to remember this night for the rest of my life, and this time there won't be any heartache attached to it. Just the connection and love of two old friends who have insanely good sexual chemistry but would never work on paper.

And I lean into it with my whole heart, taking everything Chase has to give me and giving him everything I am in return.

CHAPTER 26

ADDISON

 # Always remember your manners

Gingerly, I slide out of bed and gather up my clothes from last night before stuffing them into my duffel bag. I sneak into the living room to get dressed, pulling on my thick leggings and jumper. I zip my boots up slowly, careful not to make any noise and wake Chase. Last night was all kinds of fun, but that's all it was. Can't let myself get caught up in thinking it was anything more.

Closure. That's what it was. And now it's time to jump in Angelina and hightail it back to Juniper Ridge to get on with my life. Picking up my case and duffel bag, I tiptoe to the door before carefully unbolting it. The hinges creak a little when I pull the door open and I wince at the sound.

And then I shriek as I'm hit by a mini avalanche.

I slam the door closed quickly, but it's too late. The hallway already looks like a snowman's memorial service. With a groan, I shake the white powder from my sheepskin boots and go to the window. I groan louder. There must be four feet of snowfall out there. I can barely see Angelina's yellow roof.

"Were you planning on sneaking off without saying goodbye, Firefly?" His voice makes my heart stutter, like someone just took a defib to my chest.

I spin around to see him leaning against the door jamb, his sweats hung low on his hips and revealing far too much of that incredibly toned body to be good for my mental reasoning.

I shrug. "You're just mad you didn't get to do it first."

His eyes rake over me, like a subtle caress on my skin. "I was never planning on walking out without saying goodbye. For the record."

The way he's looking at me has heat blooming between my thighs, and that does nothing to ease my temper. Why is the universe doing this to me? I had this all worked out. I was supposed to be up and out of here before he even woke up. I was supposed to make it at least appear like last night was as casual for me as it was for him, and now it's all shot to hell, and I simply look like a pathetic little girl who couldn't even get this one thing right. That's not exactly his fault, but it's my anger that fuels my response to him. "No. Sneaking off to fuck someone else while I'm sleeping is more like your style, huh, Chase?"

The change in him is instant. The lazy grin that seems to be permanently on his face around me vanishes to be replaced with a dark scowl. This is dangerous Chase. The one who Jasper met last night. Don't fuck with me or I'll put you in the ground, Chase. He pushes off the doorframe and stalks across the room, like a sleek panther headed for its prey. "Watch your mouth, Addie."

I'm so shocked I actually gasp out loud like a moron. Watch my what now? "Who the hell do you think—"

I don't finish that sentence. Can't actually, because Chase's strong fingers are cupping my jaw and holding my mouth open. "You don't get to speak to me like that, Firefly. You don't get to pretend you don't have feelings for me after what we did."

I wrench my jaw from his grip. "Are you serious right now? That was just sex, Chase. Two people can have sex without there being feelings involved, and you should know that," I snap.

He leans closer, invading every inch of my personal space and setting all of my nerve endings on edge. "People don't do what we did last night without feeling something for each other."

My body wants to lean into him, reminded of how well we fit together, but I fight it and keep my chin tipped up while I glare into his ice-blue eyes. "Well, that would require you having some kind of feelings for me now, wouldn't it, and we both know that's not true."

He growls, like a possessive dog who just got back his favorite chew toy and doesn't want to let it go, and then the maniac hoists me over his shoulder and walks back to the bedroom.

"Chase! Put me the hell down."

That demand only earns me a sharp crack on my ass.

"Chase!"

He tosses me onto the bed then kicks the door closed behind us. "Let's get one thing straight, Addie, I have feelings for you, okay. So many fucking feelings that they're driving me to distraction. I don't know which way is up or which is way is down." He reaches for my right foot and yanks off my boot before tossing it over his shoulder.

Okay, of course he has feelings. He's not a robot. But that doesn't change anything. "What do you think you're doing?" I attempt to inject some authority into my tone, but it's a feeble protest and predictably he ignores it and pulls off my left boot.

"The snow is four feet thick, Addie, and it's still coming down. I checked the weather. It's not melting for days. You and I aren't going anywhere, baby."

"So what? You think I'm just going to fall back into bed with you because I have nothing better to do?"

He arches an eyebrow. Cocky son-of-a-chipmunk! "No." He drops to his knees and then slowly starts peeling off my socks. Then he presses a kiss on the inside of my ankle that sends a lightning bolt of pleasure right to my core. "But I am going to teach you some manners, princess."

What in tarnation! "Manners?"

He rolls off my other sock. "That's what I said." Then he winks at me and my heart stops and starts again. I don't know what's happening here. This seems playful and intense, and too much but not enough. Chase Hunter is undressing me, and not like last night when I decided to have a fuck-it moment and throw all sense out of the window. This is Chase admitting he has feelings for me, and we both know I have far too many for him, not all of them positive. This means something and I don't know if my poor, bruised heart can take it when this inevitably ends. I could handle it when it was on my terms, but now it feels like he's very much back in control. Ordinarily, it's exactly what I like in a guy. Someone who'll take charge and give me exactly what I'm craving, something which has been sadly lacking in my recent relationships. But with Chase...he has everything I've ever wanted. Everything I need, but he also has my heart and I'm not sure I can give him any more of myself and walk away unscathed.

"Chase?" My voice breaks and my lip wobbles.

It stops him in his tracks and he rocks back on his haunches. "Do you want to leave, Firefly? I will shovel all of that snow away with a spoon if that's what you really want."

My heart is hammering so hard in my chest I'm sure I'm going to have some kind of cardiac event. "That would take forever."

"I'll give you forever too if that's what you want."

No! He can't say things like that. He can't make me promises that he can't keep. He can't keep making me fall in love with him. "You're not playing fair."

"Addie," he says my name like a prayer, so reverently it's enough to pull me out of my spiral. My eyes find his gaze and he's staring at me, with a mixture of concern and hunger. "I know that I really fucked up, Firefly, but

I'm not that guy anymore. I would never fucking hurt you. Never."

"I want to trust you, Chase."

"So, take a leap of faith with me, baby. I won't screw this up again."

A leap of faith! Is life even worth living without a little faith? I can't ignore the effect he has on me even after all this time. My body practically sings whenever he's anywhere near. Despite our past, every single guy I've ever dated is measured against him, and they always fall short. He only has a hand on my ankle and my entire body is trembling, aching for his touch.

I swallow my nerves and take a leap. "Teaching me some manners, you say?"

His blue eyes light up with desire. "You sure you want this?"

I nod. "Do we need a safe word?"

"No, baby. You want me to stop at any point and you tell me so, okay?"

Every nerve ending in my body is already tingling with excitement. "Yes." I might live to regret this. Chase Hunter was my first mistake, but also by far the best mistake I ever made.

CHAPTER 27

ADDISON

 # Always show the appropriate respect for snow (and for dominant demigods with a spanking kink)

How did I end up here again? Naked and bent over Chase Hunter's lap, my bare ass up in the air while he spanks me? Teenage me would be so excited for us. Twenty-seven-year-old me is currently so turned on and desperate for him to fuck me, I'm writhing on his lap and mewling like a sex-crazed she-cat.

"Your ass is stunning, Addie. My red handprints all over your soft skin make it even prettier than usual."

"Stop teasing me," I snap.

He brings the flat of his palm down hard on my ass cheek, and it makes a satisfying cracking noise against my flesh. "I've hardly even started, baby."

Another smack, before he rubs his strong hand over the skin, soothing the stinging. "But you're taking your spanking so fucking well."

Crack!

"Ow," I whine, wriggling my ass, desperately trying to tease him so that he'll snap and just bang me senseless.

"That didn't hurt," he laughs before smacking me again. "I barely touched you."

It's true, it doesn't hurt. Not really. A mild stinging, usually followed by Chase's soothing hand. I've been spanked plenty of times before, but in the middle of sex. Not like this. Not like where the spanking is *the* event.

"I wish you *would* touch me," I say, pouting.

He cups my jaw, twisting my head so I'm looking up at him. "Spanking your ass already has me harder than titanium, Addie. You'll be getting fucked when we're done, baby, so stop pouting."

Oh, hell in a handcart! My insides just turned to molten lava, and I'm pretty sure I'm already dripping down my legs. Like he's reading my mind and wants to confirm that, Chase slides a thick, delicious finger inside me. My back arches on a moan.

"Soaked already, Addie. I think you're enjoying your spanking, aren't you?"

I press my lips together, refusing to confirm and he smacks me again, a little harder. "Or do you want me to stop?"

I shake my head. "Don't stop," I mutter.

"What, baby? I didn't hear you."

Asshole! "Don't stop!"

He hums softly to himself. "Yeah, I thought so."

He keeps that one digit inside me, not moving, while he goes on spanking me.

"Your pussy squeezes me so tight when I smack your ass. So fucking tight."

I moan, wetness slicking his finger, and then he starts moving it and the wet, filthy sounds of my arousal are unmistakable.

"Addie," he groans. "I knew you were a little brat, but you're really fucking enjoying this, aren't you?"

I press my face into the duvet and moan my agreement, my cheeks flushing with shame and desire.

"I love it too, baby. You feel how hard I am for you?" He takes my hand and places it over his cock, which is indeed thick and hard and the thing I want inside me very soon.

I squeeze him over his pants and he groans, "I'm desperate to fuck you, Firefly, but first you're gonna promise me to never try and sneak out on me without saying goodbye again, aren't you?"

"Yes, I promise," I whine, desperate for him.

He spanks me then soothes, over and over again, relentless and persistent. "Why were you trying to leave?"

Tears are rolling down my face, but I still don't want this to stop. It's deliciously sexy and naughty, and I love his hands on me. "I wanted to be the one to walk away this time."

He brings his hand cracking down over my ass cheek and I wince. My ass is getting sore now and I'm reaching my limit. And then both of his hands are gently rubbing my stinging flesh, soothing all of the soreness away. "I'm never walking away, Addie. Okay?"

I sniff. "Okay."

"Good girl," he says softly, and I bask in the bliss of his praise.

Then he slides out from under me, leaving me on all fours. I already know what's coming and my pussy clenches in anticipation at the thought.

He climbs behind me on the bed, hands tightly gripping my waist. "You look fucking incredible right now." He sinks himself inside me in one long, deep thrust, filling me so completely that I almost melt into the mattress. If he wasn't holding me up, I'm sure that I would. "Fuck, baby. So fucking good," he growls.

All I can do is whimper at this point, whimper and take every punishing thrust as my orgasm builds to a crescendo, and the smooth bastard talks me through it, telling me how amazing I feel and what a good girl I am.

Okay, so I think I love snow. I mean I always liked it, but now it's responsible for me being trapped inside this sex cabin with the machine of a man currently railing me like our lives depend on it.

Yes, I love snow.

I also love Chase Hunter, but we already knew that, didn't we?

CHAPTER 28

CHASE

 # Toys are teammates

"Fuck! Fuck! Fuck!" I grumble.

"Wi-Fi dropped out again, huh?" Addie says, an amused grin on her face as she sashays past me wearing only one of my T-shirts and a pair of my socks, which almost reach her knees. I'm going to assume she's not wearing panties since she declared she only brought enough to last her four days—a situation I have zero complaints about. But I do really need to send these revisions for the Dallas building to my assistant today, so as tempting as my little siren is, she'll have to wait for now. Although a part of me would like to abandon all hope of ever getting a strong enough signal and follow her to wherever it is she's currently headed, but I tell my dick to quiet down and let me work.

I curse and reboot my laptop another six times before I finally get some signal again to allow me to send my document to Keeley. And then I go in search of my girl. When I find her in the sex dungeon, the rush of blood to my cock almost stops my heart.

"What are you doing in here, Firefly?"

"Just looking. Don't tell me you're one of those guys who gets intimidated by a few toys in the bedroom, Chase? They're not competition, you know?" The smile she gives me is wicked and sinful.

I come up behind her, sliding my arms around her waist and pulling her juicy ass against me until it's perfectly nestled against my cock. "I don't get intimidated by anyone or anything, but I'm not sure how wise it is to use any of the things in here."

She laughs. "You were always a little anal about using other people's stuff."

I smack her ass. "Forgive me if I don't want my girl using secondhand butt plugs."

She snorts a laugh that has her perfect ass rubbing against my dick and making me harder than iron. "Not butt plugs, Chase. They don't have those kinds of toys here for obvious reasons."

I wrap her long hair around my fist and pull it to the side, giving me access to her neck, before I trail my teeth over her sweet-scented skin. "Good to know. If you need *any* toys, baby, I'd be happy to buy them for you."

"Ooh," she says with a soft sultry purr. "And exactly what kind of toys would you like to buy me? Apart from butt plugs, which you seem to have a thing for?"

I slip my hands beneath her oversized T-shirt and squeeze her ass. "You were the one who mentioned anal. And no, I don't have a *thing* for butt plugs, although I definitely have a thing for your butt. Would you wear them for me, Firefly?"

She hums softly. "I think I could be persuaded to."

"And then would you let me fuck your ass?"

She presses said ass into my hands. "Oh, I could definitely be persuaded to do that."

My hands glide over her hips and up her rib cage, until I'm cupping her perfect tits in my palms. I squeeze them gently until she moans. "And I'll definitely buy some nipple clamps for these."

"Oh, Chase," she purrs, rubbing that juicy ass over my aching dick. "What if I told you I have some here with me?"

She has nipple clamps! My dirty, dirty girl. I sink my

teeth into her neck and groan, "Then I'd ask you why the hell you didn't tell me this two days ago, baby."

She laughs, the sound soft and sexy. "I honestly forgot about them. I have a vibrator in my bag too."

"Addie!" I groan her name. "Did you use it when I was sleeping on the couch? Tell me you fucked yourself with it while you were thinking about me?"

"I didn't. But I have done before. Plenty of times."

"What the fuck are you trying to do to me? I'm gonna need you to go get your toys and meet me back in here."

"Seriously?" she giggles.

I smack her ass hard. "Seriously."

CHAPTER 29
ADDISON

 # Always stay appropriately hydrated when engaging in strenuous activity

T'm practically lit up with excitement as Chase inspects my nipple clamps, running the chain through his strong fingers and humming appreciatively. "These are gonna look so fucking pretty on you, Firefly," he growls.

I bite down on my lip, unable to speak. He places them in the pocket of his sweatpants and then stalks toward me. "Arms up," he commands.

Without question, I obey and he gently peels his T-shirt over my head and drops it to the floor. Then he slips his hand between my thighs, teasing me for a few seconds before he pulls away. "I love the no-panty look on you, Addie."

"Thank you," I whisper.

His hands glide over my hips and then along my rib cage before he palms my breasts, squeezing them gently. "These were fucking made to be played with, you know that?" Before I can answer, he dips his head and sucks a hardened nipple into his mouth, swirling over the bud with his skilled tongue and making me moan.

Wordlessly, he pulls the clamps from his pocket, his eyes burning into mine as he fixes the first clamp to my left breast.

I sink my teeth into my lip again as the bite of the clamp sends a current of pain through my chest.

He arches an eyebrow. "Okay?"

I whimper and nod. The pain is already giving way to a deep, aching pleasure.

He clamps my other nipple and this time I cry out.

"Oh, baby, they look so fucking good on you." Gently, he tugs the brass chain that holds them together, sending shock waves of pleasure rippling from my breasts to my core.

"They feel so good," I whine.

SADIE KINCAID

He hums, eyes raking greedily over my body. "Go kneel in front of the mirror."

I swallow hard, trying to get a handle on the endorphins racing around my body, and then I do as he asks. The clamps do look beautiful actually, the way my swollen nipples are peeking out between the teeth and the delicate brass chain hanging between my breasts. It's like a piece of erotic jewelry. But quickly, my eyes are drawn back to Chase and I watch his reflection as he undresses silently. Then he grabs my vibrator from the dresser and stands behind me. Wow, he really is spectacular, every muscle in his body rigid and toned, and his cock—also rigid and weeping precum.

He kicks my ankles further apart. "Those socks are fucking criminal on you, by the way. You should be spanked for making me hard wearing them like that."

I flutter my eyelashes. "Sorry, sir."

He smirks. "Brat."

Then he drops to his knees behind me. "Look at how beautiful you are, Addie." I stare at him in the mirror and he cups my jaw and tilts my head. "No, look at you, not me. Tell me you're beautiful."

I've never thought of myself as unattractive, but it's difficult to admit that I'm beautiful. He makes me feel it though. "I'm beautiful," I whisper.

"Louder," he commands.

218

"I'm beautiful!"

He plants a kiss on my temple. "Good girl." Then without warning he pushes my vibrator inside me and switches it on. My whole body starts shaking again. "That feel good?"

I nod. "Uh-huh."

He pulls on the chain between my breasts, sending more pulses of ecstasy through me. "You still think I'm intimidated by your toys?"

"No," I whimper.

"I like fucking you with this." He drives the vibrator in and out of me. "I might buy you a bigger one though, this is pretty small." He laughs, and the sound is dark and dangerous.

It is small compared to him, but he already knows that, so I don't feed his ego any further by saying it out loud. His free hand alternates between toying with the chain and then my clit as he slowly and expertly drives me to the brink of ecstasy.

"I like watching you in the mirror, Addie, but I really need to taste you too."

And now he's rolling me onto my back, his head moving between my thighs before he sucks my swollen, needy clit into his mouth. One hand moves the vibrator in and out of me and the other glides over my stomach, before he takes hold of the chain and begins to tug gently, up and down, to the same rhythm as he's fucking me. And I can barely hold on. Barely breathe. A raft of erotic sensations washing over and through me, over and over, relentless and euphoric.

"Chase!" I whine, needing him to stop and keep going. Because something intense and unfamiliar is building inside me, and it's scary and exciting all at once.

"Come for me, Addie," he groans, the vibration of his mouth pulsing through my clit. And whatever the feeling is, I can't hold back for a second longer. My orgasm comes in a rush of liquid heat and I vaguely hear the sound of something wet hitting the floor as my heartbeat pounds in my ears and I experience the most intense orgasm of my life.

I pant for breath, my entire body shaking, and I know what just happened and I can't quite believe it did.

"Fuck, baby," Chase groans, lapping at the arousal still dripping from my pussy while he slips the vibrator out of me.

I dare to lift my head. "Did I just..."

He flashes me the cockiest grin I have ever seen. "Yeah, you did."

I blow out a breath. "That has never happened to me before."

His grin grows wider, even more smug than it already was. Then he pushes up onto his forearms, his wet mouth planting kisses over my skin and covering me in my own cum. He flicks his tongue over my swollen nipples and I whimper involuntarily.

And then his forearms are either side of my head and the evidence of what he just did to me is literally staring me in the face. I'm all over him. "You can stop smirking like that," I tell him.

"I just made my girl squirt for the first time in her life. I don't think I'm ever gonna stop smiling again."

"Like your ego needed any inflating."

He winks, so sexy it's not fair. "Let's find out just how wet I made your needy little pussy, shall we?"

He sinks his thick cock inside me and the growl that rumbles in his throat makes me giggle. I snake my arms around his neck. "I know you made me squirt, but do you feel how hard I make you, Chase?"

"Yeah, I do, baby. So. Fucking. Hard." He thrusts into me on every word to drive his point home.

I love the effect I have on this man. No one before him has ever made me feel so empowered, so desired. Even though he likes to take control, he still manages to make me feel like I have it all. How much control will I have when this is all over though, and he has to go back to LA?

CHAPTER 30
CHASE

 # Always end meetings with your colleagues in a respectful and professional manner (unless you find yourself in extenuating circumstances)

"So, we'll have the final plans drawn up for Monday for your approval," Claudia says and then she outlines some of the projects my junior associates have been working on. I listen, glancing at the clock on the wall. I promised Addie I'd be an hour at most, and already this meeting has taken three. But the Wi-Fi is working like a charm today and I'm taking full advantage while I can. Still, I'll have some serious groveling to do by the time I get off this call.

"Are you about ready for something to eat?" Her soft, sultry voice makes my head snap up.

Holy. Goddamn. Motherfuck! My mouth drops open and I don't even bother to hide my reaction from my VP. Without returning my eyes to the laptop screen, I cut off Claudia mid-sentence.

"I gotta go. We'll talk tomorrow." I snap the laptop closed.

Addie giggles. Siren!

"Addie." Her name comes out as a fucking groan and I let my eyes rake over every single delectable inch of her body. From the slutty red heels that she already knows drive me crazy, up her long-toned legs to the barely-there red lace panties, which is all my girl is currently wearing as she leans against the doorframe. My gaze wanders higher, over her stomach before they linger on the most perfect tits I have ever had the pleasure of seeing in my entire life. Her nipples already sitting up and begging for attention. The kind I'm more than happy to provide.

I move my laptop to the table. "Come. Here."

She laughs. "So bossy in your shirt and tie, but I like it."

She struts across the floor, hips and ass swaying

seductively, rocking the heels like she came out of the womb wearing them. As soon as she's within touching distance, I grab her wrist and pull her onto my lap. "You're really fucking naughty making me end my meeting like that."

She flutters her dark lashes at me. "I only asked if you were ready to eat."

"Hmm." I run my nose over her neck. "While offering up something you know I find impossible to resist." Sliding my hands up her rib cage, I cup her breasts and squeeze until she moans. "These are fucking perfect, baby. Just look at the way they fit in my hands."

She arches her back, pressing herself into me, and I dip my head and suck one of her delicious nipples into my mouth. "Chase, you're so good at that."

Flicking my tongue over the stiff peak, I smile when her moans grow louder. "You're so fucking sensitive. It's not hard to get you all worked up."

She huffs a self-deprecating laugh. "You should try telling most of my ex-boyfriends that."

"They were all assholes," I growl, not wanting to think about any man but me ever having his hands on her.

"Jasper loved my boobs though. If only to jerk off on them. It was his favorite thing."

I nip her hard, because Jasper is not welcome here in

this conversation. "The fact that he preferred to come on your boobs instead of inside you only solidifies my previous assessment that he's a grade-A douche-canoe."

She links her hands behind my neck. "Well, I never let him actually do that, remember. For that, there's only ever been you."

I was obviously referring to him doing that with a condom, but I still love the reminder that I'm the only man to ever take her bare. I growl, my grip on her tightening. Possessive need flares hot in my chest. I slide my free hand into her panties, my fingers slipping easily through her wet folds. "Why are you already soaked, baby?"

She hums softly, her eyes holding mine. "I was reading a book while you were in your meeting. I found it on the bookshelf in the dungeon. Unsurprisingly, it was a very spicy story."

"Maybe you can read some of it to me later." I push two fingers inside her tight heat and immediately her pussy walls squeeze around me. "And just to be crystal clear, I am the *only* man who will ever come inside you. Ever. I'm the only man who'll ever touch you again." I sweep my fingers over the spot inside her that makes her mewl like a kitten. My sassy little Firefly, always so soft and submissive when I have my hands on her.

She doesn't argue with me, too busy riding my fingers. She probably has no idea yet how much I mean every word I just said. "Did they have any lube in that dungeon?"

"Y—yeah."

I growl, overwhelmed with the need to come in every part of her. "I'd really like to bend you over the end of this couch and fuck your ass, Addie. Would you be down for that?"

The way her eyes blow wide and her pussy squeezes around me, I'd say she sure as fuck was, but I still wait for her reply. "Yes."

"Good girl." I continue working my fingers inside her, delivering her the orgasm I've already started off.

I lay her down on the couch when she's done and go grab the lube. The bottle is sealed, which is reassuring, and when I get back into the living room, she's already lying on her front with her ass on display for me. Something about the way the red lace of her thong disappears between her cheeks does something feral to me. I climb on top of her, pulling her long, dark hair out of my way so I can pepper her back and shoulders with kisses. "Have you had sex like this before?" I ask, wondering how much prepping she'll need.

"Yeah."

I push myself up onto my knees and tap her juicy ass. "Bend over the arm of the couch for me then."

She does as she's told, wiggling that perfect peach seductively as she does. I leave her thong on and pull it to the side and then I coat two fingers with a generous amount of lube.

"Spread your legs for me, baby."

She shuffles her knees apart, the tips of her heels grazing my thighs and her ass opening up for me, until I can see her pretty hole. The couch creaks as I move between her legs, sliding my finger over her entrance and pushing gently past the tight ring of muscle.

Her back bows as she moans softly.

"That okay?" I check in with her.

Her confirmation is a soft, sultry "yeah" that spurs me on. Her ass squeezes me tight as I push all the way to the knuckle, twisting and opening her up for me. When she groans with pleasure, I take it as my cue to add a second. I push past the resistance until I have two fingers knuckle deep inside her.

"You still feel good, Addie?"

She nods, gasping. "Yes, Chase. I'm ready."

"Ready for my cock?"

"Please!"

Holy fuck! If anyone had told me at the start of this week that Addie Kinsella would be bent over a sofa begging me to fuck her ass I would have told them they were insane. And yet here we are, her pushing that juicy ass back for more and my cock aching to be inside her.

I add plenty of lube to my shaft. Despite knowing how much she wants this, I'm still nervous about hurting her. So, I add a generous squeeze of the lube to her asshole as well, and she squeals at the cold gel on her skin.

"Sorry, baby." I grab hold of her hips and nudge my crown at her entrance. "I don't want to hurt you."

She glances over her shoulder and gives me a sexy smile. "I know you won't. I trust you."

It's her trust that really unravels me, even more than her sexy body. Even if I don't deserve it, I'll take it anyway. My eyes roll back when I push gently inside her, and her ass muscles clamp around the tip of my cock. There's no chance in hell I'll be able to bottom out inside her, but even if I don't, this is enough.

"Chase!" she cries out in pleasure.

"My cock in your ass feels good?"

"Yes! Yes!" she chants.

"Rub your clit for me, I want to make you come like this."

Always obedient when I'm fucking her, she does as she's told. Her hand snaking between her thighs. I'm not going to last long with the way she's squeezing me, so I keep a tight grip on her hips and slow my movements. Just long enough until I feel her on the edge with me. And when she comes, the vibrations from her pussy rippling travel to my cock and I sink deeper, harder.

"Fuck, Addie." I empty myself inside her, endorphins charging around my body. And I stay inside her for a few moments, planting kisses on her back and enjoying the sensation of my warm cum filling her ass.

"That was intense," she murmurs.

"Yeah," I agree. Then I pull her to lie down beside me on the sofa, envelop her in my arms and rest my lips on the top of her head. "Thank you."

"No, thank you," she laughs softly, burrowing into my chest. "Who knew me wearing nothing but my heels and panties would get you so riled up?"

I resist the urge to swat her ass and instead pull her closer. "Seeing as how I spent three hours in my meeting today instead of one, I think I owe you. How do you feel about a soak in the bath while I make dinner?"

The sound that comes out of her sounds like a cat purring. "I feel all kinds of happy about that kind of evening."

"Good." I kiss the top of her head. "As soon as I can feel my legs again, I'll go run you a bath."

She rubs her cheek against my chest. "Don't rush. I like it here."

Yeah, I like you here too, Firefly.

CHAPTER 31

CHASE

Always remember where you left her panties

The loud banging on the door startles us both.

"Addie!" Brax calls.

She sits bolt upright. "It's Brax."

I rub my eyes and try to remember where we are. Oh, yeah. She told me how she'd always had a fantasy about having sex in front of a roaring log fire, so we brought the duvet and pillows and all the blankets we could find out here and then I made her dream come true. Twice.

"I'm coming. Give me a minute," she calls out,

scrabbling around for her clothes, but she's not going to find them. I undressed her in the bedroom.

She finds my T-shirt and yanks it over her head. "Where are my panties?"

I lie back with my arms behind my head. "In the bedroom."

She glares at me. "Why are you just lying there so casually? Why aren't you freaking out?"

"I think you're freaking out enough for both of us, baby," I tell her.

She shakes her head, staring at me like I'm insane. "That's Brax outside. My brother. Your best friend."

"And we are two very grown adults, Addie. Two adults who are here in this cabin because of him."

"Ugh!" She jumps up. "Please just put some clothes on."

"Well, you're wearing my T-shirt, and you used my shorts to wipe up the pool of cum that came out of you when I made you squirt, because you were too embarrassed to just enjoy the moment." I wasn't. I basked in that glory for as long as she'd let me.

Her cheeks flush the most adorable shade of pink I've ever seen.

"Addie! Chase! Are you okay?" Brax yells.

"Yeah, we're coming, buddy. Give us a second," I call out. Then I jump up and pull her into my arms.

"I will go put some clothes on, baby, but there is no hiding what we've been doing in here the past four days. The entire cabin smells of sex."

She looks horrified. "It does not."

I nod. "Yeah, it does."

"I need to crack a window."

It will take more than a window, but I don't tell her that because she's already panicking. "Brax is going to be fine about this. He loves you. He knows you're an adult and as long as you're happy, he'll be happy. But in the unlikely event that he's not, then I will take all the heat for this. I promise you."

She screws her eyes closed. "I know he'll be fine, if not a little shocked. I'd just rather it didn't look like we'd been having sex in here all night when he walks in."

"Got it." I scoop up the pillows and covers and carry them into the bedroom. Then I toss her panties and jeans out to her before I pull on some shorts. A minute later, we're ready to open the door to Brax.

The wait alone means he already knows what was going on. He's not stupid.

He's standing beside Eva, each of them holding giant snow shovels. "Busy, were we?"

"Hey, you put us in a cabin together," I remind him.

He brushes past me and hugs his sister. "Are you

okay? Did he make you do anything freaky that you didn't want to do?"

"What? No!" Addie snaps.

"Then, just know I'm not choosing sides if you ever break up." He turns to me now, his face serious. "Unless you cheat on her or break her heart, and then I'll bury you." He holds up the shovel like he means it.

"I won't do either." At least not for a second time.

"I knew you two had feelings for each other. I've been saying that all week, haven't I, Brax?" Eva says, muscling her way in and wrapping an arm around Addie and me. "I'm so happy for you both."

"That explains why you're not mad then?" Addie says.

"That and our pact," Brax replies.

Oh, shit! The pact. The one I didn't keep my end of.

Addie frowns. "What pact?"

Brax sits on the sofa and grins. "The year after you went to college and I noticed the way Chase started looking at you different—"

"What? He did?" Addie interrupts him.

Brax nods, grabs a handful of almonds from the bowl on the coffee table and tosses one into his mouth. "Yeah, he did, and I made him promise that he would never make a move on you unless it was because he wanted an actual relationship. No casual hookups allowed. And he promised, because he would never fuck up our friendship for a hookup, right buddy?"

"Yeah." Technically, I'm not lying. I had no intention of *just* hooking up with Addie. After we spent the night together, she was mine, as far as I was concerned. Pity I conveniently forgot that meant I was hers too.

I watch her face going through a range of emotions and wonder if this is when she's finally going to come clean and rat me out, but she doesn't. Instead, she flops onto the sofa next to her brother. "So, tell me how married life has been."

Brax gives Eva a look that makes her blush.

Addie pulls a disgusted face. "I mean, minus the sex, obviously."

"We just got married and we've been snowed inside a fucking cabin for four days, Addie, that's pretty much all married life has been like."

I suppress a smirk. Pretty much all non-married life has been like too. And as relieved as I am to get back to the real world, I'm also really fucking sad that this is going to end. Not that Addie and I will end. I'd seal us up inside this cabin forever before I let that happen.

Addie shakes her head like she's trying to forget what he said. "So, tell me how and why did you get out?"

Brax points to the snow shovels. "Josh and Dad

brought us these and then Dad sent us to help dig you and Chase out. The roads are clear, and we're driving back home this afternoon."

I see the crestfallen look on her face and I know it's because she's thinking the same thing as I am, that this idyllic love-in is over. Her being sad about that makes me happy even if it also makes me an asshole.

"So, everyone is headed home today then?" she asks.

Brax nods. "Mom and Dad are packing up now. Dad said if you couldn't get your car out and you want them to wait for you, then they will, but I told them you'd be fine."

"I'm sure Addie and I can take care of her car," I assure them.

"I guess we should get packing, angel." Brax stands and holds his hand out to Eva. "I know the shop is bursting with cars waiting to be fixed."

"You sure you two don't need any help?" Eva asks.

Addie gives her sister-in-law a hug. "No. We've got it covered."

"The hotel owner told us all the cabins have been freed up until the weekend, so take whatever time you need."

It takes us at least another ten minutes to say our goodbyes, and Eva, Brax and Addie make plans for donuts and coffee in their favorite bakery on Sunday, and I try not to be too butthurt about the fact that I won't be there to share it with them.

As soon as she closes the door after them, she spins around and fixes me with one of her infamous glares. "So, you had a pact?"

I slip my arms around her waist. "In my defense, when we slept together, I had every intention of making it much more than that. I never once considered you a casual hookup, even if my actions said otherwise."

She hums, eyes raking over my face, no doubt she's considering how to make me pay. But instead, she smiles and leans into me. "I'm going to miss this place. I'm going to miss you."

I tuck a strand of hair behind her ear. "I'm going to miss you too."

She sighs, pressing her cheek against my chest. "I guess we should start clearing that snow, huh? And then we can get back to our lives."

I have never wanted anything less in my entire life. "Stay with me one more night, Addie."

It takes her a while to answer, and it feels like an eternity before she does. But then she looks up at me, her lashes wet with tears. "Okay."

I kiss her tears away. I have to make this work, because losing her now would kill me.

CHAPTER 32
ADDISON

 # Always say a thorough goodbye

We went to the main hotel earlier, and we said another goodbye to Brax and Eva and to my parents. Then Chase booked his flight and I called Emma and told her I was sorry, but I'd be back home tomorrow. As usual, she was cool, because she's awesome, but it made me realize how much I've missed her—and my little store.

These past eight days have been incredible, but it's not my life. It's a fantasy, a wonderful one though, and one I'll continue to enjoy for every single second that it lasts. Because thinking about tomorrow when we're going to have to say goodbye is too painful to contemplate right now.

Chase cooked dinner for us, pasta with some dried mushrooms and pancetta, and we finished off the final dregs of bourbon as we washed up after. And now we're sitting here across the kitchen table, staring at each other in silence like this is our first date. I feel nervous for reasons I can't explain.

"You ready for bed, Firefly?" he finally speaks.

I nod, nerves and excitement fluttering low in my belly.

He pushes back his chair and then takes my hand before leading me through the cabin. Once we're in the bedroom, he undresses me slowly, trailing kisses over the skin he exposes. "You are so incredibly fucking beautiful, Addie," he groans as he crouches down onto his heels to pull off my jeans. Then his hands glide up the outside of my thighs, to my panties. Torturously slowly, he peels them down my legs before helping me to step out of them. His nose rubs over my pussy and he growls, feral and unrestrained. My knees tremble.

He glides his palms up my inner thighs and I part my legs for him, allowing his fingers to slip through my slick center. "And this pussy is so fucking sweet, Addie."

He swirls his tongue over my clit. "Do you have any idea what you do to me, baby?"

I thread my fingers through his hair and rock my hips against his mouth. "No."

"You drive me fucking crazy." He grunts before picking me up and tossing me onto the bed.

And then he undresses for me. Revealing his thick biceps and the toned muscles of his chest inch by inch. And when he pushes his jeans down over his solid thighs and lets his thick cock bob free, I suck in a stuttered breath. Something about this feels different. Maybe it's because this will be the last time we do this, maybe ever. His life is in LA, and mine is not.

When he's naked, he crawls over me, peppering kisses over my skin until he reaches my neck. I wrap my legs around his hips and pull him closer, until the thick crown of him is nudging me open.

"You want this, baby?"

"Yes, please." I arch my back, needing him inside me.

He sinks inside me in one smooth thrust. "Then it's all yours, Addie. I'm all yours."

"And I'm yours, Chase." I wrap my arms around his neck, prepared for him to rail into me the way he usually does, but instead, he slowly rocks his hips, sweeping the tip of his dick over a sweet spot deep inside me that has every cell in my body trembling.

"Oh, God."

"Not God, Addie. Only me." He pulls out and sinks in deeper, making my eyes roll back in my head. "You take my cock so well. I love how deep I can get inside you like this."

"So deep," I whimper.

"Yeah," he growls before sinking his teeth into the base of my neck.

Pleasure coils deep in my core, spiraling through my limbs and back again. White-hot fire and ecstasy permeating through every cell of my body, and all he's doing is fucking me to a slow, relentless rhythm and growling filthy things in my ear.

"Listen to how wet you are for me. You love my cock, don't you?"

"Yes!" Starlight explodes in my vision and I rake my nails down his back, bucking my hips to take more of him.

"Addie," he growls out my name, finally picking up his pace as he thrusts inside me, until we both hurtle over the edge together.

He stays inside me, each of us panting for breath as we come down the high. Then he rests his forehead against mine. "I love you, Addison."

My heart practically bursts with happiness, but what if none of this is real? I don't trust my instincts where he's concerned. "That's just the orgasm talking."

"I know you make me come pretty hard, baby." He moves inside me and aftershocks of pleasure pulse through my core. "But I'm still in full control of my senses. I fell in love with you a long time ago, Firefly, and I never fucking stopped."

"So, why didn't you ever come back, Chase?"

"You threatened to stake me if I ever did, remember?"

"Like you ever let anyone tell you what to do in your whole life?"

"Nobody except you it seems." He kisses me softly. "But I didn't come back because I knew how much I'd hurt you, Addie. And you were right about so many things, about how I was wasting my life—"

"I had no right to say any of that to you."

"Yeah, you did. And it was the kick in the ass I needed. Because of you I finally stopped thinking about what I wanted to do and I made something of myself. And I didn't want to come to Juniper Ridge until I was the man you deserved. I'm not sure I'll ever be good enough to deserve you..."

"You are, Chase."

"I really want to be, Addie."

"I've been in love with you for as long as I can remember. I don't think I ever stopped either."

"We'll make this work, I promise. I can't lose you again."

I really want to believe him, but I'm also a realist. Chase's life in LA is as important to him as mine in Juniper Ridge is to me. How are we going to combine the two successfully and not resent the other for it? "I don't want to lose you either, but we live on opposite sides of the country."

"I'll find a way to make it work, baby. I promise. Do you trust me?"

I stare into his deep blue eyes and know there's only one answer. "Yes, I trust you."

He seals his lips over mine and then he kisses me like it might be the last time we ever do this, even if we both hope that it's not.

CHAPTER 33

CHASE

 # Never make promises you can't keep

I t fucking kills me to say goodbye to her. To stare into her tear-filled eyes and make a promise that I have no way of proving I'm going to keep. I asked her to trust me and I believe that she does, but I have a sinking feeling she's thinking I'm going to fly back to LA and forget all about her.

"I'll call you as soon as I land, okay?"

She nods, biting down on her lip.

"You and Angelina be careful driving back, won't you?" She's a perfectly good driver, swerving into Kelly's

Superstore aside, but I'm still going to worry about her until she's home safe.

That at least gets me a smile. "We will. Say hi to Faraday for me, won't you?"

I laugh, knowing I will never not see that car and call it that now. What the hell has she done to me? "Yeah, I will."

She sighs and rests her forehead on my chest, and I tip her chin up with my pointer finger until she's looking up at me once more. "We're going to make this work, Addie."

"I know. When will I see you?"

I swallow down the knot of guilt. "I'm going to try my best to get to Juniper Ridge for New Year's. I have a huge project that I have to get wrapped up and I'm going to be working all over the holidays."

"I know. Me too. Christmas is our busiest time."

"We'll make it work."

"Yeah, sure."

I fucking hate the way that she says it like that. I know it will be hard, but people have long-distance relationships all the time.

My Uber pulls up and I wrap her in my arms and kiss her so hard, she'll still feel my lips on hers until I see her again. When I get into the cab, she waves me off, a smile on her face even though I can see the tears rolling down her cheeks. I hate this, but I have a life and responsibilities in LA that I can't just leave behind.

As soon as I landed three days ago, I headed straight to my office and I've barely left since. The Dallas job has been taking up way too much of my time, not to mention some headaches popping up from a project that was completed weeks ago. But some asshole got a copy of some building code regulations he says we're in breach of, even though I know for sure we're not. Still doesn't stop the asshole trying to screw us over though.

Keeley pops her head into my office. "You asked me to tell you when it was six o'clock."

Shit! I did. I can't believe it's already that time—the time I agreed to call Addie. I hate these all-too-brief calls, especially when she always sounds so sad when they end. It's not enough. Never enough where she's concerned. And at the end of every call, I wind up feeling guilty as hell that I'm not giving her enough of my time.

"You also have that new meeting scheduled in ten minutes," Keeley reminds me.

Fuck! Addie was right. This long-distance thing isn't going to work. My job is my whole fucking life. I don't know when that happened, but it did. Like it or not, I can't live this life and have her too. No matter how much I might want to.

CHAPTER 34

ADDISON

CHRISTMAS EVE

Red flags are green if you squint in just the right way

It's been twelve days since Chase left for LA. We spoke every day for the first six days, although each call got progressively shorter and shorter. Usually, he'd call me first, but then it was me calling him. And then he'd be in a meeting and would promise to call me back, and the time between missing my call and returning it would get longer as the conversations got shorter. Always rushing off to another meeting or to fix something.

I can't blame him. I knew this long-distance thing

wouldn't work. He's too busy for a relationship with someone living in the same state as him, never mind someone living on the other side of the country. We haven't spoken at all in two days now. Just a text from him this morning telling me he loves me.

I'm sure that's true, but sometimes love isn't enough.

My mom steps back from the Christmas tree, clapping her hands and admiring her handiwork, and deservedly so.

"It looks beautiful, Mom."

She wraps her arm around me, her eyes shining with delight. "It always reminds me of you kids and how excited you used to get. You always used to love Christmas."

Her expression turns sad when she looks at me. "And then, it seemed..." She tucks a lock of hair behind my ear. "For a while, it seemed like you stopped."

I hug her tightly. "I still love Christmas, Mom," I assure her. Now is not the time to think about Chase Hunter. I've forgiven him for breaking my heart all those years ago, and even though it's breaking again right now, that's not on him. I'm sure he really did want this to work as much as I did.

The doorbell rings.

"I'll get it," Eva shouts, followed by the sound of her stockinged feet scampering down the hallway.

The door opens and she shouts again. "Addie. It's for you."

I look at Mom and she shrugs, like she has no idea who would be calling here for me either. Only Emma would drop by to see me, and she's definitely in Chicago based on the thousands of photos she keeps posting to her Instagram page.

I walk out into hallway, passing a grinning Eva on my way. She's closed the door on whoever is out there and I can't help wonder if this is some kind of surprise my family have cooked up. A Christmas singing telegram? Carolers? A pony? All of the above?

I pull open the door and my heart stops beating. Because it's better than all of the above by a country mile. "Chase?"

He smiles and those mesmerizing blue eyes twinkle brighter than Christmas lights. "Hey, Firefly."

"W—what are you doing here?"

"I told you I was going to make this work, didn't I?"

"I know you said that, but..."

He frowns. "You didn't believe me?"

"Not exactly. But what about your job? You've been so busy."

He takes my hand and pulls me out onto the porch

and the doors close behind me with a soft click. Then he opens his thick wool coat and wraps it around me, until the two of us are inside it and I'm squished up against his chest. "There's a reason I've been so busy, baby. I'm sorry I wasn't able to talk as much as I wanted to, but I had to tie up a few loose ends before I could get here."

That makes my heart hurt for him. "I love that you did that, but I don't want you killing yourself just to be able to spend a few days here with me."

"I'm not here for a few days, Firefly."

Now my heart hurts for me too. Not even a few days? "So, how long are you here for?"

He runs his nose over my jawline, a deep animalistic growl rolling in his throat. "I don't want to spend another second of my life without you in it, Addison Kinsella. I love you. Always have. Always will." He presses a soft kiss on my lips and I melt into him like the snow in the first rays of the winter sun.

"I love you too, Chase. But...you live in LA."

"I'm moving home to Juniper Ridge—"

"No, I can't ask you to do that."

He chuckles softly. "You didn't ask me, baby. Did you even hear what I said?"

I did. He called Juniper Ridge home. "You actually want to move back here?"

He nods.

"But what about your job? Your clients?"

"I've had a reshuffle. Promoted a couple of my best project managers to VPs, so I can take more of a back seat and focus on the design, which is the part I love anyway. But that's where we might need a little compromise, Firefly."

"What kind of compromise?"

"You're going to have to move too."

I blink. "Me move? But if you're coming home to Juniper Ridge, and I already live here, why am I moving?"

"I can work remotely for the most part. There'll be a little travel involved when I inspect sites, but most of what I do I can do from anywhere. Most of my clients already travel across the country for my services. It shouldn't matter if they have to come to LA or Juniper Ridge. But for that I'll need an office space. And ideally one on Main Street. And there are none available right now."

"I still don't understand."

"I wondered if maybe you'd be willing to share yours?"

"You want my store?" Technically, he owns it so he could take it if he wanted to, although I know he never would. But I rack my brain for how we might make that work. We're so short of space already and Emma and I work hard to make the best of what we do have. It's perfect as it is, but for him...I guess I can make room, seeing as he's moving his entire life for me. "We could move some stock upstairs, I suppose."

Chase shakes his head. "I would never ever ask you to give up your store, and I made sure your lease is iron-clad, baby. Nobody could ever take it from you. But I was thinking more like the space above it..."

"You mean my apartment?"

"Yeah."

"But then where would I live?"

He squeezes me tighter. "With me, I hope. I bought the old Cooper place."

My mouth drops open. The one I told him I dreamed of living in, with the wraparound porch and the swing and the huge field out back with space for chickens and dogs, and lots and lots of children. "You bought that? But how? When?"

"Closed yesterday. I'll be moving in after New Year's. And you don't have to move out right away. I'll have a home office that I can work from for as long as I need to. You can take all the time you need." He cups my jaw between his thumb and forefinger. "But not too long, because you *are* mine, Addie. You were mine from the very first time I kissed you, and you'll be mine until the day I die."

My knees tremble and if he weren't holding me up, I'm sure I would crumple to the ground in a heap. "Let me get this absolutely straight. You're telling me you're moving back to Juniper Ridge, you bought my dream house *and* you want me to move in with you?"

"In a nutshell, yes."

Wow! Arrogant, possessive, making-a-hell-of-a-lot-of-assumptions asshole. And I love him for it. "You know you're a walking red flag, right?"

"So I've been told."

A smile tugs at my lips. "What if we drive each other crazy living together?"

He kisses me again, a dark laugh tumbling out of him. "Baby, you drive me crazy every second of every fucking day and I wouldn't have it any other way. It's one of the many, many reasons I adore you." He glances over my shoulder at the window. "You know they're all watching us, although I'm sure they think I can't see them."

I can just picture the four of them peeking out from behind the curtain—their faces a mixture of shock and excitement, and I can almost hear the excited giggles from my mom and Eva. "Then you'd better unhand me, sir, or Brax and my daddy might come out here with a shotgun and run you out of town."

He hums, like he's thinking. "Yeah, they might if I

hadn't already told them I was moving back here, and that I was madly and hopelessly in love with you."

"They all knew about this before I did?" I would poke him in the ribs, but I'm too warm and comfy wrapped up in his arms.

"I asked them to keep an eye on you and let me know if you were freaking out about us. I know you'd never have told me anything was wrong. It killed me being in LA and barely being able to talk to you."

"So, this is it? You're back for good?"

He nods.

"Won't you miss LA?"

"LA is just a place."

"A place that's been your home for the last eight years."

He tucks a strand of hair behind my ear and squeezes me tighter. "You're my home, Addie. I would live in the Arctic circle in an igloo as long as you were with me."

"I think the Wi-Fi there might be terrible and then you'd be super grumpy."

He hums, running his nose over my throat. "If your parents and your brother weren't watching, I would put you over my knee right here, Firefly."

I shiver. "Don't tease me. We have to stay here at my parents' house tonight. No spanking allowed."

He smiles against my neck. "I can wait for that. But you're gonna have to learn to be quiet for me, baby, because it's been twelve very long days and I'm probably going to combust if I don't get to fuck you very soon."

"Well, I can't have you exploding in your pants at the dinner table now, can I?" I snicker.

He nips my neck. "I just added another twenty strokes to your spanking."

Sounds incredible. I press my lips against his and we kiss like we might never stop. Little does he know I plan on adding at least another hundred or so to that spank counter before we go back to my apartment tomorrow.

And I cannot wait.

CHAPTER 35

CHASE

The best things come in threes

She wraps her fluffy red scarf around her neck and smiles sweetly. "Ready?"

I slide my hands over her hips and onto her ass, careful not to squeeze too hard given the spanking I just doled out. But she deserved that—every single time she did something to drive me purposely crazy at her parents' house last night and again this morning. "How do you look so damn sweet and innocent when just half an hour ago you were bent over my lap, creaming all over my fingers while I spanked your beautiful ass?"

"I guess I'm just inherently those things," she purrs, fluttering her long, dark lashes.

"Sweet, most definitely. Innocent, absolutely not."

She gasps, feigning her outrage. "How dare you, sir?"

I press my lips against hers and kiss her, and she melts into my arms like she belongs there—which she absolutely does. "I will never get used to being able to kiss you whenever the hell I want."

"I do enjoy being kissed whenever you want. But where exactly are we going when it's Christmas and we have my entire apartment to ourselves."

"We're going to see our new house."

"It's your house, Chase. Even if I do move in."

"It's *our* house. Do you have no grasp of the laws of our country?"

"Yes. And property is nine tenths of it, apparently."

"And as my wife, you'll own half of whatever I do."

She sputters, her eyes practically bugging out. "Your wife?"

"Your parents would probably be pissed if we're not married when we have kids."

The look on her face is priceless, a mixture of shock, amusement and indignation. "So, we're having kids now too?"

"Why else did we buy the big house with the porch swing and enough room for kids and dogs?"

She grins wickedly. "And chickens."

I kiss the tip of her nose. "Whatever you want, Firefly."

NEVER IN THE history of time has there ever been anything more spectacularly joyous to watch than the look on Addie's face when I open the front door of our new house and switch on the light. She steps into the hallway, mouth open as she heads straight for the staircase in the center, running her hands along the smooth, polished banister.

"Wow!" is the only word she utters for a full minute while she explores the downstairs area. That's until she squeals with joy upon seeing the large, open-plan kitchen and living space at the back. "This place is beautiful, Chase. I knew it was gorgeous from the outside, but...wow!"

I walk up behind her, circling my arms around her waist. "You like it, baby?"

"I love it."

"You wanna spend the rest of your life with me right here in this house?"

She spins in my arms, tears shining in her hazel eyes. "Are you sure this is what you really want, Chase? You have a whole life in LA."

"No, I have a job in LA. But my whole life is right here, in my arms. I know you're worried that I'm giving something up, but I'm really not, Addie. I'm finally getting everything I ever wanted. You were always meant to be mine, and we were always meant to be right here."

"But what about the people in LA who care about you?"

I have a couple of friends in LA that I'll miss, but I spent eight years without my three closest friends in the world, I'm sure we'll all survive. "They can visit us, or we can visit them if you'd like. But every single person I love lives here in Juniper Ridge."

"Will Faraday be coming?"

I can't help but smile at her name for my car. "Yes, he's being delivered next week, and he's very excited to meet Angelina."

"I hope you told him Angelina is a classy lady, and she won't be impressed by his huge engine or his horsepower."

I pull off her scarf and run my nose over the back of her neck. "I bet you will be though. I can't wait to take you for a drive in him. Maybe we could go somewhere secluded and we can test how comfortable his back seat is."

She spins in my arms and pops an eyebrow. "Don't you know already?"

Minx! I trail my teeth over her sweet-smelling neck and resist the urge to bite. "No. I do not."

There's a wicked glint in her eyes, the kind that's probably about to earn her another spanking. "Angelina's back seat is very comfy, by the way."

A possessive growl rumbles deep in my chest and this time I do bite her, making her squeal and giggle. Then I lift her onto the counter and wrap her legs around my waist. "And why on earth would you think I'd want to know that, Firefly?"

"In the event you'd ever like to christen her with me. I only know she's comfy because Brax and Eva picked me up from a bar in her once."

My eyes narrow on her pretty face. "You knew exactly what I'd think you were talking about though." I nip her again. "Siren."

She hums softly. "You're very hot when you do that possessive, jealous thing."

"It's not a thing. It's how I feel when I think about anyone but me touching you." I unbutton her coat and pull it off her. "I really fucking love that I was your first, Addie." I tug off her boots and jeans.

"But know that I'm gonna be your last too." I pull her panties to the side and sink two fingers inside her.

"We shouldn't do this here," she whimpers.

"Why not, baby? It's our house. And you and I are going to christen every single surface of it. Starting with this counter right here."

Her arms snake around my neck and she tips her head back, riding my fingers. I work her over until she comes hard, screaming my name all over the kitchen.

When she stops trembling, I slide my fingers out of her and kiss her forehead. "There's my good girl. So good, I think Santa might have even left a gift for you upstairs."

Her eyes widen. "Here? For me?"

"Yeah." I didn't have time to buy her anything but some perfume and chocolates at the airport for Christmas. But the gift upstairs, I ordered for her as soon as I got back to LA.

"But I didn't get you another gift."

She gave me a beautiful set of monogrammed cufflinks this morning, and a belt which I will absolutely use to tie her up with later. "I already have everything I could ever want right here."

I pick her up, legs still around my waist and carry her upstairs into the main bedroom at the front of the house. We walk into the closet and I switch on the light and set her on her feet.

She gasps when she sees them sitting on the floor, all six of them sparkling in the electric light. "Are they..." Her hand flies to her mouth. "Gianvito Rossi Ranias?"

I'm thrilled she recognizes them, but of course she would.

"You got me..." She kneels on the floor and picks up a silver shoe, running her fingertips over the sparkly fabric. "You got me a pair in every color, Chase."

"I couldn't decide which ones I wanted to see you in the most."

She rolls into a sitting position and sinks her teeth into the luscious pillow of her bottom lip. "Do you have a preference which pair you'd like me to try on first?" She's only wearing a sweater and her panties, which have a damp spot at the apex, and the sight of her stretching out her toned legs already has my dick aching to be inside her like my fingers just were.

I clear my throat. "The silver are fine."

She slips them on. "They fit so perfectly."

I reach for her hand and pull her up and she gives me a twirl. "How do they look?"

Fucking incredible. "I'm not sure. I think I need to see them as they're supposed to be worn."

"You mean like with a dress or something?"

"No, baby. I mean like take everything off except the heels."

Her eyes sparkle with desire and excitement. "Oh, you want to see them like that?"

"It's why I bought them for you."

"Then it would be rude not to give you what you paid for, sir," she purrs before peeling off her sweater and letting it drop to the floor. Next comes her bra, and she peels it languidly down her arms until her full tits spring free. I have to stop myself from pouncing on her already.

She turns in a circle, giving me a spectacular view of her ass. "Panties too, Addie."

Torturously slowly, she hooks her fingers into the waistband of her panties and then works them over her hips and thighs. When they fall into a pool of damp fabric at her feet, she expertly steps out of them before flicking them at me with the point of her shoe.

My fingers curl around the delicate lace and I hold them to my nose, taking a deep inhale that has me feral for her. "Fucking delicious," I growl.

"Is this what you wanted, Chase?" She spins in a circle again, and I lose all the control I've been holding onto. I push her against the dresser while pulling my cock from my jeans and then I practically mount her.

And she wraps her legs around me and sinks the heels of her shoes into my ass.

"*This* is what I want, baby. What I always fucking want. You. Naked. And my cock inside you."

"God, Chase, you're so good at that," she groans, hands fisted in my hair. "And thank you, by the way."

I drive into her. "Do you mean for the shoes or the fucking?"

She giggles and it lights me up from the inside. "Neither. I meant for you."

I smile against her skin, pulling her closer and tighter, until there's not a sliver of light between us.

I forgot how much I love Christmas, and by the next one she's going to be my wife and then I truly will have everything I've ever wanted.

EPILOGUE 1

ADDISON - SEVEN MONTHS LATER

Happy endings should always be delivered as promised

"Take it all off, Firefly. Leave the shoes," Chase growls. He's sitting against the headboard in his shirt and dress pants, arms behind his head and his biceps straining against the fabric of his shirt. He looks good enough to eat.

"You want me to leave the shoes?"

He nods. "I love fucking you in those slutty red heels."

I gasp, faking my horror. "Pretty sure you're not allowed to call your wife slutty, sir. Especially not on her honeymoon."

"Pretty sure I called your shoes slutty, baby. Now take off your clothes and get your ass over here."

"The dress too?" I lower the straps of the beautiful cream silk dress he bought me today while we were shopping in Milan. The one that hugs my curves so perfectly it feels tailor-made, and the one he's been growling about tearing off me all night.

"Especially the dress. I want to see what's mine."

I unzip it agonizingly slowly.

He growls, frustrated. "Don't make me come over there and rip it off you, Addie."

"You can't do that, Chase. It cost a fortune. And I did promise you a striptease."

He groans, "You're all tease and no strip."

"You're so impatient."

He climbs off the bed, stalking toward me like a lion stalking its prey. "No, Firefly. I have been a very patient man. I have taken you for dinner and danced with you under the stars, and I have behaved like a gentleman all night while you have flaunted this incredible, sexy body every single chance you got."

He slides his arms around my waist, yanking me close until my chest bumps against his. "Hmm." I trail my fingers over his collar. "I'm not sure sliding your hand into my panties in the car, or following me into the restroom and pinning me against the wall while you fingerbanged me can be considered gentlemanly behavior."

He smirks, pulling my bra down and exposing a hard nipple. "Given what I wanted to do to you, I'd say it was pretty damn restrained." He dips his head and sucks the stiff peak into his mouth. I arch into the pleasure, moaning softly as his skilled tongue works over my flesh.

"You're always so sensitive here, baby," he chuckles before tugging down the rest of my bra and paying the same attention to my other breast.

No, I'm not sensitive, he's just too skilled. I'm like Silly Putty in his hands—or his mouth. "I didn't take my birth control today."

He nips me gently and a feral growl rumbles in his chest. "Good girl."

We both want kids—he wants two, I want four, but maybe we'll compromise on three.

With skilled fingers he works my dress down and over my hips, until the fabric lies in a cream pool at my feet. His hand glides over my stomach, and then dips into the waistband of my panties. Pleasure is already skittering around my body before he even touches me, and then his fingers brush my clit and I groan his name.

"Sensitive here too, princess. You know these

panties are soaked." He slides his hand all the way inside them.

"Because you made me come in the restroom, and the car," I remind him.

He smiles against my skin. "You make it very hard to keep my hands off you, baby. Very. Fucking. Hard." He punctuates the last three words with a kiss, working his way up my collarbone to my neck.

I squeeze the length of him through his pants. "Yes, I'd say you definitely are."

He captures my wrists, circling them both in one strong hand before pinning them behind my back. Then he runs his nose over my neck, humming softly to himself. "You had your chance, Addie, and now it's my turn to play."

He tweaks my nipple and a shiver of excitement runs up my spine. "What exactly do you have in mind?"

A dark laugh tumbles out of his lips, his breath warming my skin. "I guess you'll have to wait and see."

"Will it at least involve lots of orgasms?" I ask cheekily.

He swats my ass hard. "Don't I always take care of you, baby?"

"Yes, you do. Always." In every single way there is.

"I love you, Addie Hunter," he growls. "Remember

that in a few minutes when I have you tied up and begging for my cock."

"I love you too, Chase Hunter."

He is the only man I've ever loved. The only man I'll ever love.

He wasn't my first mistake—he was never a mistake at all. But he was my first everything.

And like he said, he'll be my last.

EPILOGUE 2

CHASE - FIVE MONTHS LATER – TWO WEEKS
BEFORE CHRISTMAS

The happiest endings usually happen twice (at least)

Addie leans back in the seat, kicking off her heels and stretching out her legs. "Don't tell Angelina, but Faraday is kind of comfortable," she says with a giggle.

"I won't tell her," I assure her. "But you do know you're going to have to trade her in for a new model soon." And by a new model, I mean a top-of-the-line SUV, which will have every safety feature ever invented.

She pouts. "But I love her. I know you think she's unsafe, but she's really not."

I rest a hand on her thigh and squeeze gently, not taking my eyes off the road. "It's not big enough for the baby carrier and all the things we're gonna need, Addie."

"I know," she says with a dramatic sigh. "But she's been with me for so long. Maybe we could keep her for when this little one is old enough to drive." She rubs her hands lovingly over her stomach. She's thirteen weeks now and showing a little.

Over my cold, dead body will any of our kids be driving that fluorescent hazard on wheels. "I think she'll be pretty outdated in seventeen years. Don't you?"

"I guess," she admits reluctantly. "It's a pity Eva can't use her."

I keep my thoughts on that to myself. Brax is as unlikely to want his pregnant wife driving that yellow death trap as I am mine.

"Can I get another yellow car?"

"Whatever you want, baby."

She peers out of the window and giggles again, a sound I will never tire of hearing. She's always laughing, smiling—happy. And that makes me happier than I ever dreamed possible. "I think I know where you're taking me, sir."

We passed the signs for Vermont a while back and I knew my surprise would be revealed then. "Where else would I take you for our anniversary, Addie?"

"Our anniversary is in July," she reminds me.

I take her hand in mine, lift it to my lips and kiss her knuckles. "That's our wedding anniversary. I'm talking about the anniversary of us getting snowed in."

"Oh, yes. That." I don't miss the way her breath hitches and it has my cock twitching in my pants. It's difficult not to think about sex when I think about the cabin, or indeed when I think about my wife.

"Are we going to Lakefisher Lodge?" she asks, excited.

"Wait and see."

"I bet we are. I wonder if they still have their sex dungeon?" She snorts a laugh and it's so sexy that I almost stop the car and fuck her on the side of the road.

"Aw, Chase it's still beautiful, isn't it?" she says as we pull up to the cabin.

"Gorgeous," I reply, but I'm staring at her.

I grab our bags from the trunk and we head inside, and when we do, I'm pleased to find the new furniture in place.

"Looks like they did the place up since last year," she says appreciatively, running her hand along the back of the new, tan leather sofa.

"Yeah."

She flashes me a huge smile. "Let's go see if they upgraded the sex dungeon too."

She sprints off to the sex dungeon and flings open the door, gasping when she sees what's inside. "Chase! You should see what they've done in here," she says, turning to me with her mouth hanging open. "It's stunning."

She disappears into the room and I follow her. The garish red walls are now painted a muted dusky pink, one of Addie's favorite colors, except for the wall that's essentially one large mirror. The windows aren't blacked out any longer, but instead they have the kind of glass that can't be seen through from the outside. And instead of a sex swing, a wooden four-poster bed dominates the room—the kind with restraints on each bedpost. Cuffs made of the softest leather—I know that because I chose the material myself. Only the best for my girl.

She walks over to the antique dresser and traces her fingers over the toys. A paddle. A flogger. A set of jeweled butt plugs. Cuffs. Nipple clamps. A wand vibrator.

"All this stuff looks new," she whispers. "They've really gone upmarket, huh?" She spins around, her cheeks flushed pink. "Maybe we could even sleep in here." She eyes the bed, clothed in three hundred count

Egyptian cotton sheets and adorned with red and pink pillows in a variety of shapes and sizes, all designed to make various sex positions easier, especially now she's pregnant.

"We can sleep in here whenever you like, baby. Merry Christmas."

She blinks. "What do you mean?"

"This is your gift, Addie."

"You bought our cabin?"

I nod.

"And had all these changes made?"

"Yeah. Everything is new. Everything is yours."

"Chase!" Her lip wobbles and her eyes fill with tears.

I wrap my arms around her waist. "What is it, baby? Don't you like it?"

"Yes. I love it." She sniffs. "But I only got you a pen and some socks. I mean it's a very fancy pen that I got engraved especially, but still…"

I know I shouldn't, but I laugh. "You have given me everything I need already, Addie. I will love my pen and my socks, and I will still act surprised on Christmas morning when I open them."

She winces now. "Sorry. I am planning on getting you something else too. I'm going gift shopping with Eva next week."

I shake my head. "I don't need anything but what I

have right here. So, can I unwrap my favorite gift right now?" I tug open the belt on her sweaterdress.

She nods, lip trapped between her teeth.

"That's my good girl." I scoop her into my arms and lay her on the bed and then I take my sweet time unwrapping her. My favorite gift I've ever gotten.

My favorite everything ever.

My wife. My heart. My home.

Want more Chase and Addie? You can download a free bonus epilogue for them Here if you're reading an ebook, or in Sadie's FB reader group if you're reading on paperback.

And if you like possessive alpha males who are teddy bears for those they love, then why not check out Sadie's bestselling Manhattan Ruthless series.

Broken

Promise Me Forever

Rebound

Played

Made

ALSO BY SADIE KINCAID

Enjoy alpha billionaires, then you'll love Sadie's Manhattan Ruthless series

Broken

Promise Me Forever

Rebound

Played

Made

Have you tried Sadie's bestselling paranormal/fantasy series yet? If you love possessive broody vampires, witches, wolves and all things magic, then try the Broken Bloodlines series here

Forged in Blood

Promised in Blood

Bound in Blood

The complete, bestselling Chicago Ruthless is available now. Following the lives of the notoriously ruthless Moretti siblings - this series will take you on a rollercoaster of emotions. Packed with angst, action and plenty of steam.

Dante

Joey

Lorenzo

Keres

If you haven't read the full New York Ruthless series yet, you can find them on Amazon and Kindle Unlimited

Ryan Rule

Ryan Redemption

Ryan Retribution

Ryan Reign

Ryan Renewed

And the complete short stories and novellas attached to this series are available in one collection

A Ryan Recollection

If you'd prefer to head to LA to meet Alejandro and Alana, and Jackson and Lucia, you can find out all about them in Sadie's internationally bestselling LA Ruthless series. Available on Amazon and FREE in Kindle Unlimited.

Fierce King

Fierce Queen

Fierce Betrayal

Fierce Obsession

If you'd like to read about London's hottest couple. Gabriel and Samantha, then check out Sadie's London Ruthless series on Amazon. FREE in Kindle Unlimited.

Dark Angel

Fallen Angel

Dark/ Fallen Angel Duet

If you enjoy super spicy short stories, Sadie also writes the Bound series feat Mack and Jenna, Books 1, 2, 3 and 4 are available now.

Bound and Tamed

Bound and Shared

Bound and Dominated

Bound and Deceived

About the Author

Sadie Kincaid is a dark mafia, contemporary and paranormal romance author who loves to read and write about hot alpha males and strong, feisty females.

Sadie loves to connect with readers so why not get in touch via social media?

Join Sadie's reader group for the latest news, book recommendations and plenty of fun. Sadie's ladies and Sizzling Alphas

www.ingramcontent.com/pod-product-compliance
Lightning Source LLC
Chambersburg PA
CBHW021219250626

47155CB00008B/2870